The Fatal Bouquet

The Pearl Hotel Cozy Mystery Series

Book 4

NANCY PENNICK

This is a work of fiction. Names, characters, businesses,
places, events and incidents are either the products
of the author's imagination or used in a fictitious
manner. Any resemblance to actual persons, living
or dead, or actual events are purely coincidental.

The Pearl Hotel Mystery Series is dedicated to my sister, Susan, who encouraged me to bring Serena to life. To my cousin, Beth, who always says yes when I ask for help. And, to my husband, Ron, who reads every word I write.

Chapter One

"Lavender." Serena huffed. "Mention that word one more time and prepare for the world's most primal scream."

Serena Tate had one heck of a week. She wished to slam her teacup onto its saucer, but instead, set it gently in place. When she glanced up, she saw her two best friends struggling to hold back their laughter. "It's not funny," she said.

"It is." Lily reached out and touched the top of Serena's hand. "We were waiting for this day to come. Five months of holding back your frustration is a long time."

"When we received the P.I.C. text, we knew it was critical. Partners in crime always respond," Mia replied, giving Serena a sympathetic look. "We promise not to say, 'I told you so'. We're here to listen."

Serena looked at Mia with affection. "What do I always say about us? How did an exceptional black woman like me, who had just turned forty, cross paths with an outstanding Japanese woman like you?" She connected with Mia's striking chocolate eyes, and her heart melted.

Although in her early thirties, Mia Takeda still had a child-like quality yet was tough and determined. Serena had written her first bestseller, *Marry Me Never*, inspired by Mia's experience with a sociopathic boyfriend. With her permission, of course.

"So true." Mia chuckled. "We decided it was fate."

"Because of Mia, I met you," Serena said, taking Lily's hand. "My beautiful, inside and out, friend."

"Don't forget tech nerd," Lily added with a huge grin.

Lily claimed she highlighted her mousy brown hair to add some wanted flair, but she didn't need to do anything to make herself shine brighter. Her personality won everyone over. Recently, she had chosen a new style of longer, layered hair that perfectly framed her beautiful oval-shaped face and proportioned lips.

"Thanks again for coming so quickly," Serena said. "When Justice asked me to help with his wedding, I said no." She gazed at her friends. "Remember?"

"Absolutely." Mia held up one hand.

"But he wore you down," Lily replied. "He played on your emotions."

Mia narrowed her eyes. "Justice knew you were the only person who could get him The Pearl's reception hall on short notice."

"True," Serena agreed. She recalled the conversation with her ex-husband.

"Please, Serena, I'm begging you. We don't have much time to find a venue. Tasha dreams of being a June bride. The Pearl is booked on Saturdays that month, but I hope you can work your magic," Justice had given her sad puppy dog eyes and a pout. That look used to work in the past, but Serena had gotten over him long ago.

At six foot three, Justice possessed a rugged bad-boy charm, which added to his attractive look. His perfectly trimmed goatee and neatly braided hair always looked as if he'd come from the barbershop. Yet looks weren't everything, and after they married, Serena saw a different side of him.

When their twin girls were born, Justice refused to change his habits or adjust to their new lifestyle. Throughout the years, Serena managed the daily tasks and after-school activities. When Justice began to skip dinners and social events, she finally had enough and filed for a divorce.

Now Justice turned to her for help. Help to marry another woman. Serena exhaled and looked at her friends. "I should have stopped when I got the month he wanted. *June*. But no. Stupid me agreed to be their wedding planner." She placed her head in her hands. "Why?"

"Because you are a kind person," Mia said.

"Plus, your girls are part of the wedding, and you want to stay informed," Lily added.

"You're exactly right, Lily." Serena dropped her hands. "I shouldn't complain."

"You convinced Justice to change the wedding to Friday, suggesting he had a better chance of scoring a date," Mia said. "Since you secured a date, Justice and his fiancée think you can do anything."

"Yeah, right." Serena gave a humorless laugh. "Actually, Tasha Harrington doesn't think I am capable of much. According to her, I couldn't hold on to my husband or make my marriage work. Of course, she says all this when Justice isn't around."

"Worst kind of people. She's nice to your face when Justice is there, then puts you down when he's not," Lily said. "I bet she would deny everything if you told Justice."

"It's the reason I've said nothing," Serena answered.

"Serena," Mia said. "If you wouldn't mind, could you tell us more about Tasha? All I know is you went to high school with her, and she comes from a rich family."

"You got all day?" Serena smirked.

"Yes, we do," Lily exclaimed, appearing eager to hear the details. "I'll ask Jun to bring us more tea and some scones."

"You had me at scones," Serena replied. She took a deep breath and gazed around The Pearl's tearoom, one of her favorite spots in the hotel.

The tearoom's moss green walls had evenly spaced cherry wood faux windows. Translucent white paper filled the window's square spaces. Matching rectangular lanterns sat in the middle of each guest's table. The designers had chosen seating from the same rich-colored wood, which cast a reddish glow. They'd placed lifelike cherry blossom trees against the walls and in strategic corners. Vertical wood beams, with gold calligraphy dancing down their centers, created a feeling of being transported to another time or place. Serena usually soaked in her surroundings, but not today. She loved the tearoom's atmosphere, yet she couldn't stop thinking of the upcoming wedding and her to-do list.

"Oolong for you, Serena," Jun said, breaking into Serena's thoughts.

"Thanks, Jun, you read my mind." Serena smiled up at the woman.

Jun, their dedicated server, and Serena had a special bond. They often teased each other, especially about tea choices. Serena insisted she ordered various kinds of tea, yet Jun always served her oolong.

Once Jun finished pouring, she asked, "Will there be anything else?" After the women responded they were fine, she left the three friends to continue their discussion.

"Tasha dated Justice in high school before we were a couple," Serena announced. "Did I ever tell you that?"

"No." Mia shook her head. "You've kept that part of your life private. May I ask why?"

"The past is unrelated to the present." Serena dropped her shoulders. "Although I'm starting to think it is."

"Did Justice break up with Tasha for you?" Lily asked, widening her eyes.

"He says no, but from the way Tasha acts, maybe he did."

"Why are you torturing yourself? Most of your bridal chores are done. The wedding is a week away. Quit." Lily stared at her through her tortoise-shell framed glasses.

"We know why, Lily." Mia giggled. "Material for her new book."

"Mia!" Serena gave her a faux horrified look. "How did you know?" She grinned.

"You finished your holiday thriller, *Behind the Nutcracker's Smile*, and you're looking for new material. Real-life experiences help the process."

"You know me well." Serena nodded.

"Can you believe this is your fourth book?" Lily asked. "Thanks for letting me read the first draft. The guy who plays the nutcracker king in your story made chills go up my spine. He's nice out of costume, but when he puts it on, watch out. Using The Nutcracker ballet for your setting was a great idea."

"Ooh, I'm glad you like it," Serena said. "I've sent it to my publisher. They want to release the book in November before the holidays. But that's five months away, and for now, I must focus on Justice's wedding."

"Then let's get back to your high school story," Mia said. "When did you start dating Justice?"

"The beginning of senior year. We'd known each other since middle school but only exchanged hellos or had brief conversations. We never shared a class until he ended up in two of mine that year. One class followed the other, so Justice joined me on the walk from first to second period."

"Aww, it sounds like a cute high school romance," Lily said. "Boy meets girl in class. They walk the halls to their next class and fall in love."

"And they didn't live happily ever after," Serena finished.

"But you have two beautiful twin daughters because of it," Mia said. "Who, may I add, just completed their first year of college."

Serena smiled as she pictured her girls. Fraternal twins. Their only shared trait was their height. Five feet, nine inches. A perfect height for modeling, which they hoped would be part of their future. Jade had gotten her father's handsome looks and rich brown skin tone, and Jewel favored Serena with her honey brown skin and golden-brown eyes.

"Yes, we were blessed with them. I can't deny it." Serena admitted with a smile.

"Tell us more about Tasha," Lily said. "Were you friends in high school?"

"Acquaintances?" Serena wrinkled her nose. "She and I had a different circle of friends. We called her group Tasha's court because she was the queen, and they all vied for her attention. Newly rich and beautiful, she could have anything she desired."

"Except Justice." Mia held up a pointer finger.

"At forty-two, she can have him." Serena chuckled. "Come to think of it, she never married. Did she wait for him this entire time?"

"Perhaps," Lily said, lifting her shoulder. "When did they start dating?"

"She insists they've dated for years," Serena answered. "I can't pin her down to an exact time."

"Ooh." Mia wiggled in her seat. "When Justice asked you to marry him again, you wondered if he had a girlfriend. Justice admitted he did. Do you think it was Tasha?"

"This gets more interesting by the minute," Lily said, rubbing her hands together. "Serena, why haven't you told us about Tasha?"

"I had no clue he was dating her until five months ago," Serena answered. "Imagine my surprise when Justice called me in January and said, 'Do you remember Tasha Harrington?' When I said I did, he told me they're getting married. Out of nowhere."

"What?" Lily responded. "He dated your cousin in December, Serena. A month later, he's getting married? It makes no sense. There must be a reason." She pursed her lips. "Obviously, Justice strung her along for years, but why marry her now?"

"I need to find out, don't I?" Serena poured another cup of tea. "What's wrong with me? I promised myself to stay away from the drama."

"You chose not to cause problems," Mia replied. "And you wanted to show the girls you could get along with Justice's fiancée. It's the reason we're here today. You can't take it anymore. So, let it out. Keep going."

Serena exhaled. "The maid of honor and one bridesmaid are from Tasha's high school court. The group has stayed in contact since graduation. Tasha's closest friend Amanda Shaw, also known as Mandi with an 'i', is her maid of honor. Or is it matron of honor?" She grimaced. "She's divorced."

"Doesn't matter," Mia said, lifting her shoulder. "Most people say, 'maid of honor'. Although it may not be correct, it's easier."

"Back in the day, Mandi was cute and full of energy," Serena continued. "She was a cheerleader. Brunette with the most beautiful blue eyes. Everyone said she should have been homecoming queen, but that honor went to Tasha."

"That didn't hurt the friendship?" Lily asked. "It *was* high school."

"Not from what I can tell. They're strong as ever," Serena replied.

"What about the other bridesmaid?" Mia asked.

"Zuri Brooks. Smart girl. She was class president and head of the yearbook. Maybe valedictorian? I forget."

"So, four bridesmaids," Mia said. "Your two girls, Zuri and Mandi. I'm surprised she doesn't have a bigger wedding party."

"Oh, she wanted twelve bridesmaids," Serena replied. "But I talked her down to four. I said it would look more elegant. Plus, Justice doesn't have twelve close friends or relatives."

"Who are the best man and ushers?" Lily asked.

"Jax, his older brother, is Justice's best man. They are four years apart and not close. Jax was in college when I dated Justice. When he graduated, he received a job offer in another state. I never got to know him." Serena checked her phone. "I'm surprised I don't have a message from Tasha. Usually, I get one per hour." She smirked.

"Okay. On to the ushers. Let's see. Justice asked his cousin Dwayne, and two friends he has stayed in touch with since high school. Jarrett and Evan."

"Hello, everyone. I'm delighted to find you here." A voice behind Serena greeted the women.

Serena instantly knew who had spoken. "Nina, won't you join us?" she asked, turning toward the woman.

"Thank you, Serena." Nina dipped her head. "I believe I will."

Nina Takeda, an impressive woman in her mid-seventies, took a seat at the table. She owned The Pearl Hotel, Serena's home away from home, and commanded attention in any room, despite her height of five feet and one inch. Her chignon bun appeared neat, and she never had a hair out of place. Nina's fashion sense always made her look runway ready. She had her nails done to perfection, never a chip or the wrong color.

"Grandmother," Mia said. "sit here." She patted the spot next to her. "If you were searching for us, it must be urgent."

"Well, not exactly urgent, but it is something I need to discuss." Nina narrowed her eyes. "Somehow, I am now involved in Tasha Harrington's wedding. I have met her parents at a few charitable events, so she felt she could call me."

"What did she want?" Serena asked.

"To inquire about throwing lavender after the ceremony instead of birdseed or rice." Nina shook her head. "I told her we don't allow rice or birdseed in the back garden."

"I am so sorry, Nina. Tasha should ask me those questions. I'll make sure she knows," Serena replied.

"It's fine, Serena. But tell her I run this hotel and am not the wedding planner."

"I will. Plus, she already asked me about throwing sprigs of lavender," Serena huffed. "I even created a sign for the basket." She blocked out the words with her hand. "Toss some lavender and good wishes on the new Mr. and Mrs. Tate."

"I like it," Lily said, then wrinkled her nose. "Why did she bother Nina?"

"Because she could." Serena rolled her eyes. "She wanted Nina to know she was *that* Harrington. Did she drop her parents' names, Nina?"

"Yes, but I already knew. Theo Harrington is one of the most prominent Black lawyers in the area."

"Wouldn't she rather people get to know her before discovering she comes from a rich family? We don't flaunt our wealth," Lily said, glancing around the group. "Or try to impress people with who we are."

Lily spoke the truth. She married a billionaire who owned a tech company. Mia hailed from the California Takedas who'd reached billionaire status decades ago. She also had a wealthy husband.

"As we said, it takes all kinds." Serena looked at Nina and frowned. "Again. Sorry."

"No need to apologize," Nina said. "Since we went above and beyond for her wedding day, Tasha is inviting Kal and me to the wedding. Her words."

"This is getting better and better." Lily raised her brows and smiled. "How can I secure an invite?"

The women laughed at the comment and finished their time at the tearoom designing ways to get Lily an invitation to the wedding.

Chapter Two

Holding her breath, Serena Tate studied the man walking toward her. His stark white coat appeared to glow under the intense lights. As he drew closer, she noticed his name, Matthew Wilson, stitched above the pocket. He extended his hand, and she willed herself to slip her hand into his warm yet slightly moist one. His lips moved, but she couldn't hear the words.

"I'm sorry. What did you say?" Serena blinked and tried to focus.

"Your husband has died," the doctor said again.

"He's not my husband. He's my ex-husband," Serena corrected.

"You must still be close if you brought him to the hospital," the doctor replied.

The man had kind eyes, blue ones, behind rimless glasses. His gray and white speckled beard caught her attention. Neatly trimmed. The way Justice always cared for his.

"We try to maintain a cordial relationship because of our twin daughters. Justice will always be a part of our lives. Well." Serena blew through her lips as a tear rolled down her cheek. "He was."

"A wonderful father." The doctor nodded as if picturing the girls with Justice.

"Not really," Serena stated. "He just came back into our lives last year. We divorced seven years ago, and he hardly saw the girls."

The doctor pressed his lips together. "Things happen after a divorce. I'm glad you worked through it, and the girls got to spend quality time with their dad before his passing."

"I wouldn't say 'quality'," Serena answered, trying not to sound snippy. "He saw an opportunity and took it." *What am I saying? The man just died.*

Dr. Wilson cleared his throat. Serena noted his discomfort as he shifted his weight, but it was her only chance to unburden her soul and confess her deepest secrets.

"What I mean to say..." Serena patted the empty spot on the bench. "Please sit, Doctor. This may take a while." She waited until he took a seat. "I wrote a book, *Marry Me Never*, and it became an instant success. Don't ask me how it happened with so many wonderful books out there." She raised her shoulders. "But that's a story for another day. I need to return to my story." She sighed. "Following six years of only seeing Justice at Christmas and the girls' joint birthday, he calls me without warning. He asks me on a date. Can you believe that?"

"Perhaps he saw the error of his ways," the doctor said as he inched away from Serena.

"Or dollar signs." Serena shook her head. "No, he has, or should I say had, an excellent job. Justice liked attention. He wanted to be in the spotlight. My newfound fame fit the bill. Then!" Serena placed her hand on top of the doctor's for effect. "He discovered the girls would model in my friend's fashion show. Mia saw their talent and invited them to walk in her charity event. *Walk.* In modeling terms, it means walking confidently up and down the runway, in case you didn't know. Since the twins weren't eighteen, I needed to give permission."

Serena glanced up to gauge the doctor's reaction, but he was gone. A red koi, wearing the same white coat, had taken his place. "Do I know you?" She studied the fish. "Is that you, Sam?"

"It's me, Serena. Keep going. Confession is good for the soul."

Serena bolted upright and checked her surroundings. "I'm home. In my bed." She ran her hand over her face. "It was a dream." She smacked the mattress. "That darn Justice. I wouldn't be dreaming you were dead if you hadn't asked…no make that pleaded with me to help you. You wanted to marry at the hotel, but five months was short notice for a sought-after venue like The Pearl. 'Please talk to Nina,' you said." She glanced around the room. "Now I'm killing you off in my dreams." She exhaled. "Or is it a sign? An omen of things to come?"

Swinging her feet onto the floor, Serena sat on the mattress's edge and stared out the window. The bright sun gleamed in the sky, signaling midday. "This is why I never take naps. I dream the entire time. Dreams," she huffed. "They start so true-to-life, you think it's real. Then you're talking to a fish. Not just any fish. It was Sam. That's one thing you don't do, Samurai, is talk. But you are a good listener."

Serena met the beautiful red koi adorned with white fins and tail over a year ago. She was standing by the pond in The Pearl's gardens when he emerged from the water, and they connected instantly. Sam could answer yes/no questions, although no one believed her except Nina and the twins. He remained elusive, and most people thought she had imagined him. Serena named him Samurai, or Sam for short. He became her confidante and sounding board when criminal cases occurred at the hotel, which happened more often than she liked. Serena didn't plan to get involved in the police cases yet somehow ended up in the middle of them.

"Serena?" Her mother's voice came through her closed door. "Are you in there? You're too quiet."

Serena rubbed her face and rose from the bed. She walked to the door and opened it. "Sorry, Mama. I fell asleep."

"I'm not surprised," her mom answered, touching Serena's cheek. "You're trying to plan a wedding and write your next book. Don't worry about the girls and their wedding tasks. That's why I'm here."

Robin Baker, Serena's mom, had moved in to help Serena until the girls left for college. The arrangement had worked so well, Serena asked her mom to stay permanently.

"Your hair appointment is in an hour," Robin said. "You wanted me to remind you."

"Thanks." Serena studied her mom, trying to see what others saw. Many people said Serena resembled her mom with their matching brown eyes with flecks of gold and flawless honey brown skin. "Natural curls this time." Serena patted her hair, wondering what it looked like after her nap.

"No matter what you do, you'll look beautiful," Robin replied.

"Moms always say that." Serena chuckled.

"Stop teasing me," Robin said. "I'm allowed to think my daughter is the most talented, beautiful, and smartest one of all."

"Except for Jade and Jewel." Serena reminded her.

"I'd never forget my two precious granddaughters." Robin wrapped her arms around Serena. "I'm happy they are home for the summer. The house feels different without them."

"We better get used to it. One day, it will be just you and me."

"And hopefully, Jack." Robin winked.

Jack Ando, Serena's boyfriend, worked at The Pearl Hotel. During the model murder case, their first meeting had happened under duress. She smiled as she recalled their first encounter.

Mia had sent Serena on a mission. She was to deliver a message to the models getting ready for the show. Screeching to a halt in front of the dressing room, Serena held up her badge to show the security person stationed at the door. The moment she had made eye contact with the man, her heart slammed against her chest. What secrets did those seductive brown eyes hold? She had wondered. Eyes that undressed her in seconds or so she thought they had. Serena guessed he was over six feet by their close proximity and couldn't help but notice the muscled arms below his short-sleeved shirt.

When she had finished her task, Serena returned to the reception hall to search for Mia. Once she found her, Serena peppered Mia with questions. She inwardly giggled as she remembered their conversation.

"The security guy at the dressing room door. Who is he?" Serena had asked.

"You mean Jack?"

"I didn't look at his nametag."

"He probably wasn't wearing one." Mia smiled. "Jack Ando works security at The Pearl. He was my grandfather's bodyguard for ten years while he lived in LA. When Grandmother and Grandfather reunited, Granddad moved back here and brought Jack with him."

"He's Asian?"

"Japanese, yes."

"Age?"

"Forty-five?" Mia lifted her shoulder and grimaced. "Married?"

"For a short time in his twenties."

"So, kids."

"No." Mia tilted her head. "Hey, wait a minute. Does someone have a crush?"

"I saw him for two seconds, but yes. What else can you tell me?"

"Not much. I am not a matchmaker or know much about those dating sites, Serena. You'd have to check and see if Jack's on one."

"Okay, answer this. Does he have a girlfriend?"

"Not that I'm aware of." Mia shook her head. "But I could find out." She'd given Serena a devious smile.

Jack didn't have a girlfriend. Serena sighed and blinked her eyes.

"Serena?" Robin waved a hand in front of her daughter's face. "Where did you go?"

"You mentioned Jack," Serena said. "It's your fault."

Robin shook her head and grinned. "I think you found the right man." She took Serena's hand. "I have something else to tell you. A delivery person from the bridal shop brought the girls' altered dresses to the house. She gave me this message. Try them on immediately and inform the shop if anything else needs to be done."

"Whoa." Serena widened her eyes. "Okay. Are the twins here? Did you give them the dresses?"

Since the girls turned nineteen in March, Serena promised to give them more freedom, but while they lived at home, they needed to leave word where they were going. For safety reasons, Serena had told them.

"Yes, they are trying on the dresses as we speak," Robin answered. "The *lavender* ones." She gave Serena a devious smile. "Your favorite word."

"I have nothing against the color, Mama."

"You've heard it too many times." Robin chuckled. "You did a fabulous job convincing Tasha to incorporate green and gold into her palette. Maybe you should add wedding planner to your resume."

Jade and Jewel's doors opened at the same time. They stepped into the hallway, and Serena gasped. "You are gorgeous."

Jade twirled in place. "I like it."

The off-the-shoulder satin midi dress flared out at the waist. A knee-high slit on the left-hand side of the skirt would make it easier to walk. Jade turned to show Serena, and the lavender material moved with her.

"Lovely," Serena said.

Jewel did not appear as happy with the outfit. She leaned against her bedroom doorframe and watched Jade model the dress.

"Jewel, how do you feel in the dress? Need any adjustments?" Serena asked.

"It's fine."

"Are you sure?" Serena squinted as she looked at her daughter.

"She doesn't want to be in the wedding," Jade answered for her. "Neither do I, but we must make the best of it.

I'm trying hard not to fight with Tasha. She acts like she knows all about Jewel and me. Even you, Mom."

"Really." Serena said in a sarcastic voice.

"Yes," Jade huffed. "She wants Jewel and I to know she grew up like we did. Tasha told us how she went to high school with you and Dad. Her dad was a struggling lawyer at the time, and her mom devoted all her time to helping him succeed."

"Whoa." Serena held up both hands. "Hold on there. Her dad may have struggled at one time but was doing well when we got to high school. In fact, they moved to Rincon Hill after Tasha graduated. It's one of the most expensive neighborhoods in San Francisco."

"Really? Is Tasha trying to get us to like her by saying she is just like us?" Jade shoved her hand on her hip. "From the stories Tasha told, her mother supported Tasha in everything she did, devoting quality time to her only child. I wonder if Tasha realizes her mom takes credit for everything." She changed her voice to a higher pitch. "Tasha never would have become homecoming queen without my help."

"Mrs. Harrington was the first helicopter mom," Serena said with a straight face. "The hovering kind. Right?" She broke into a smile, but her girls just stared at her.

"Or maybe she needed to get a life," Jewel grumbled. "Or a job to occupy her time."

"Have you met her?" Jade wrinkled her nose. "She would never consider working. It's beneath her. She dedicates herself to charitable causes. It's her calling, as she likes to say." She rolled her eyes.

"Girls. Stop. Show some respect." Serena folded her arms over her chest. "You only have five days before the wedding, and you won't have to deal with Shari Harrington again." She had to admit defeat. "But you're right. Shari is a bit much."

"A bit?" Jewel widened her eyes. "I've learned more about her life in the short time I've known her than Grandma's. Sorry, Gram, I would love to hear more."

"I understand," Robin answered. "Shari likes to talk, and you're supposed to listen. She knows nothing about you, I bet."

"She barely knows our names," Jade replied. "But calls us her grandchildren."

"What?" Robin's face hardened. "How dare she?"

"Mama. Remember? Respect?" Serena reached for her. "Just ignore her." *Time to change the subject.* "I saw Lily and Mia this morning. They'll be at the rehearsal. Won't that be fun?"

"As guests?" Jade asked.

"No, they're helping me finalize details. Lily wants a sneak peek of the wedding, and Mia will help me oversee the decorations in the hall. Flower placement, table settings and the like."

"Wait until Tasha sees Mia," Jewel said. "She'll go crazy. We did as you asked, Mom, and never mentioned her. Although I'm sure Dad has."

"Thanks, girls," Serena replied. "Your dad may have mentioned our friendship, but I never confirmed it. Tasha may wonder if he told the truth and was afraid to ask me." She giggled. "It will be fun to see what happens when she sees Mia Takeda, one of the most popular fashion designers, at her rehearsal dinner."

Chapter Three

Serena walked into an empty reception hall with Mia and Lily. "Good. Everyone is outside. Randi has kindly offered to oversee the rehearsal and appears to have everything under control. I had no clue how to conduct one."

Randi, The Pearl's event coordinator, had helped Serena many times in the past, and Serena considered her a friend. She watched Randi direct the bridal party like a seasoned traffic cop and smiled. Mrs. Harrington tried her best to interfere, but Randi was not having it.

"Ooh, I can watch everyone, and they won't know," Lily said. "Let me guess. The thin, blonde, white woman is Shari Harrington."

"Yes," Serena answered. "And she's wearing white. What was she thinking? Only the bride should wear white."

Shari wore a fitted one-shoulder white dress that ended below the knee. The enormous bow on her shoulder caught Serena's eye. *Is she trying to overshadow the bride? Look at my dress instead of my daughter.*

"Tasha doesn't need to worry about her mom or the outfit she's wearing. The bride definitely stands out," Mia said. "The dress is designer. I love she kept her hair natural, long and wavy. She looks gorgeous."

Serena had to admit that Tasha wore the perfect dress. The white floral three-tiered lace dress had a nude color underlay, making her appear ethereal, as if she had stepped from a mythical land. Her warm beige skin tone complimented the outfit even more.

The bridesmaids wore floral jacquard fit and flare midi dresses in different colors. Jade had selected muted gold, while Jewel preferred fern green. Serena searched for Zuri and Mandi to see their color choices.

"Hey." Lily tapped Serena's arm. "The woman in the purple dress is Mandi, right?"

"Yes," Serena replied, following Lily's pointer finger until she spotted her. Mandi's long brunette locks shone in the evening sun as she laughed and talked. Serena thought she hadn't aged a day since high school.

"She appears to be a little intoxicated," Lily stated, then added. "Already."

"Do you blame her?" Serena giggled.

"Serena." Mia folded her arms. "Keep your detective hat on. You promised to evaluate the situation and get some answers. Why did this marriage happen so quickly? Are they marrying for the right reasons?"

"If I discover anything, and I mean uncover any secrets or lies, I'm not stopping the wedding," Serena said. "The show will go on."

"If you say so," Mia smirked and gestured toward the garden. "It looks like you need to start your investigation. Those two bridesmaids don't seem happy with each other."

Serena forced herself to look. Mandi and Zuri, in lavender, appeared to be fighting. "Not my problem."

"You're the wedding planner," Lily said. "Better get out there. If anything, do it for Jade and Jewel."

I'm sure it's nothing." Mia rolled her eyes and pointed toward the tables. "We'll check the place settings while you're gone."

"Fine. I'll go out there if you insist," Serena huffed.

"We do." Lily appeared to suppress a smile.

Serena strolled into the garden acting casual, although she felt quite the opposite. She headed for Randi and the women surrounding her. "Hello, everyone," she said in the happiest tone she could muster. "How is everything going?"

"We should get started," Randi answered, widening her eyes so only Serena could see. "We had to work out a few last-minute details."

Serena glanced toward the men who stood away from the women, beers in hand. They wore pale green linen dress shirts with khaki pants. Except for Justice. His clothing was all white. She cleared her throat. "Gentlemen?"

"Serena! Good to see you," Jax, Justice's older brother, welcomed her with open arms after parting from the group. He resembled Justice but didn't possess the swagger his brother had.

Why is the oldest boy always the shortest? Or so it seems. Serena shook her head to rid the thought. "Jax, it's nice to see you." She hugged him.

"Can I get one of those?" Jarrett walked up to them.

"Wow, Jarrett, I haven't seen you since…"

"The divorce?" Jarrett raised an eyebrow.

"Yeah. That." Serena chuckled. "If you'll excuse me, I need to get this rehearsal started. Jax, since you're the best man, get those men in line." She headed toward Mandi and Zuri. "Are you ready?" she asked them.

"If this brat would stop bossing us around, we could have finished the rehearsal a half hour ago," Zuri answered. "She's acting as if she's the bride."

"I am not." Mandi narrowed her eyes. "You are."

What are they? Five? "Hey, how long has it been?" Serena asked, hoping to distract them. "I haven't seen you since…"

"High school," Mandi responded in a sarcastic voice. "As if you didn't know, Serena. Oh, wait. You were too busy trying to get Justice to marry you."

"What?" Serena took a step back. "I don't think it's proper to discuss the past on a day like this."

"Right." Zuri snorted. "It's a *wonderful* day."

Not her too? "Regardless of what you think of me or this wedding," Serena said. "I would like you to line up in the order you were given so we may begin."

"Aren't you going to make one more pass at the groom before it's too late?" Mandi asked, pulling Serena aside.

Serena could smell the alcohol on her breath. *Wine?* "Mandi, are you okay?" she whispered.

"If you mean, can I hold myself together as the love of my life marries another woman?" Mandi blinked back tears. "Yes."

Serena inhaled. "Are you speaking about Justice?" *You've got to be kidding? Was I clueless during high school? Everyone was in love with Justice?*

"Who else?" Mandi widened her eyes. "He *is* the groom."

I'm going to hate myself for asking but here goes. "Did you ever date him?" Serena held her breath in anticipation.

"He walked me home after we danced throughout the night at a middle school party. Justice never took his eyes off me." Mandi sighed. "When we reached my house, he kissed me. My first kiss. I thought we'd be a couple. But no. When I arrived at school on Monday, all he said was, 'Hey, Mandi.'"

Serena bit her lip to keep her thoughts to herself. *Typical middle school boy.* "Sorry," she said.

"Do you want to know what made it worse?"

I'm all in. No backing out now. "Sure," Serena answered.

"He was walking Zuri to her class. Zuri!" Mandi tilted her head toward the woman. "The school brainiac. At the time, I didn't know he was using her to do his homework."

Sounds like Justice. "You thought they were a couple," Serena said.

"So did she," Mandi cried. "And never let me forget it."

Mandi still holds a grudge from middle school? "Don't you think it's time to let the past go?" Serena asked. "Like the song says? Let it go?" When she got no response, she said, "It's time to rehearse, Mandi. After rehearsal, I'll get you a nice strong cup of coffee."

* * * *

Dinner had finished, and dessert was about to be served when Serena noticed Jade was missing. Heading out to the hallway, she heard her daughter shout from the bridal room.

"I'm not Jewel. My name is Jade."

"You shouldn't yell at me, Ms. Jade Tate," Tasha cried. "I'm going to be your stepmother. Show some respect."

"My sister and I already have a mom. Her name is Serena Tate," Jade shot back, her voice tinged with anger. "Stop asking me to do things for you. It's the matron of honor's job."

You tell her, Jade. Serena swelled with pride as she entered the room. Jade could hold her own. "Jade, there you are. And Tasha." She lowered her lashes. They're about to serve dessert." She glanced away from her daughter and locked eyes with Tasha. "Oh. Am I interrupting something?"

"I asked Jade to come here so we could speak in private," Tasha answered. "Tomorrow is an important day, and I want everything to be perfect."

"Tasha asked me to show Mandi and Zuri how to walk, Mom," Jade huffed.

"What's wrong with that?" Tasha flipped her hand over, palm side up. "Jade is a model. She could help them."

"It's a wedding, Tasha. They're fine with the way they walk. Plus, I don't think they would appreciate advice from a nineteen-year-old," Serena replied. "Anything else?"

"She doesn't trust Mandi anymore, especially after the toast she gave tonight." Jade stared at her mom with wide eyes.

"Ah, yes, the toast." Serena closed her eyes and pictured Mandi, who had refused the coffee, wobble to her feet and gush about Justice. She spoke mostly of him and informed Tasha of her good fortune.

"Mom? Does Dad buy the bridal bouquet?" Jade asked, interrupting the scene in Serena's head.

"Yes, I believe he paid for all the flowers," Serena answered.

"Since Tasha doesn't want him to see her tomorrow, she wants me, his daughter and closest thing to him, to present the flowers to her."

"That doesn't sound so terrible, Jade," Serena answered. "You can manage carrying a flower box into this room."

"See. Even your mom agrees." Tasha linked arms with Jade. "Let's get back to the party." She brushed past Serena as if she wasn't there.

"I'll be there in a minute," Serena said in a feeble voice, holding up a pointer finger. She took a breath and sat in the nearest chair, gazing up at the ceiling. "Help me through the next day, please."

Serena drew in a breath and slowly released it. Rising to her feet, she headed back to the reception hall to find Mia and Lily waiting at the entrance. "Everything okay?" she asked them.

"Tasha finally realized Mia was here," Lily said under her breath. "She was so wrapped up in herself, she hadn't seen her."

"What happened?" Serena whispered.

"Tasha rushed up to her screaming that Justice was right. You are friends with the famous fashion designer, Mia Takeda. She couldn't believe it. Mia graciously shook hands and spoke with her for a few minutes." Lily dropped her shoulders. "She got an invite to the wedding."

"Not you? We'll see about that." Serena searched the room for Tasha. She waved when their eyes connected.

Tasha, noticing who was in Serena's company, hurried over. "What can I do for you?" she asked in a sweet voice.

"I heard you met my friend Mia," Serena said.

"Yes," Tasha squealed. "Mia Takeda, fashion designer extraordinaire. Why didn't you tell me?"

I didn't want Mia involved in your wedding or have you ask her to design your dress. "Why would I?" Serena stared at Tasha until she squirmed. "Tasha, I would like you to meet my other friend, Lily Nichols. Her husband owns Nicholworks."

"Ooh, a popular company," Tasha said, taking Lily's hand. "Did I invite you to the wedding?"

"No." Lily shook her head.

"I invite you now." Tasha looked at Serena. "Put your friends on the guest list with a plus one and let catering know."

"Sure." Serena balled her hands into fists. "Anything you want, Tasha."

"I believe they are serving dessert," Lily said, gesturing to the server pushing a cart.

"I better get back to my table," Tasha replied. "Please, enjoy the rest of the night on me." She floated among the tables, smiling and waving until she reached Justice. Wrapping her arms around his neck, Tasha kissed his cheek before taking her seat.

"Nicholworks, Serena?" Lily pursed her lips as she glowered at her.

"You wanted an invitation, didn't you?" Serena teased. "Mia?" She touched her friend's arm. "You're awfully quiet."

"Just taking it all in, Serena." Mia exhaled. "Something doesn't seem right."

"You warned me to keep my eyes open, but I see nothing that suggests a problem. Everything seems fine, aside from Tasha pushing me to my breaking point." Serena tried to smile yet couldn't.

"Let's start with Justice. Look at him. Does he appear to be a man in love?" Mia nodded toward him.

"He's overwhelmed," Serena answered.

"Mia's right. I feel it, too," Lily said. "Maybe you're too close to the situation, Serena. Usually, you're the first one to spot trouble."

"I *do* spot trouble, Lily. And her name is Tasha. But she's not my problem, she's Justice's."

"See." Lily shook her finger. "That's exactly what I mean. You're ignoring the signs. You think once the wedding is over, you can get back to your life. I'm not so sure."

"Will you two stop?" Serena asked. "You're scaring me." She scanned the room, hoping something would jump out at her. *Nothing.*

"We should start filling up your murder board with suspects," Mia said.

"What?" Serena took a step back. "No one will die at this wedding, trust me. I had Jack double the security team."

When the first murder occurred at the hotel, Serena had hung a corkboard in her office, determined to solve the crime. Finding photos and information on the internet, Serena put all pertinent material on the board. She'd used it twice more since then and didn't want a repeat performance.

"It's still on the wall in your office, right?" Mia grimaced. "We have two unhappy bridesmaids already. Who else could we add?"

"Jade." Serena hung her head and retold what happened in the bridal room.

"Don't forget you," Lily said, pointing to Serena. "The ex-wife and the woman Tasha forced to be her wedding planner."

"Forced is a strong word, Lily. She gently coerced me." Serena joked. "Besides, I'd only be a person of interest. I've been on my best behavior." She suddenly felt defensive. "Now, if you'd excuse me, I have something to check on before tomorrow's ceremony."

* * * *

"Justice?" Serena found him at the bar. "Can we talk?"

"What's up?" Justice's eyes appeared glassy, but Serena chose not to lecture him on drinking.

"I want to discuss the flowers," Serena answered. "Did you order everything, even the bridal bouquet?"

"Especially the bridal bouquet," Justice snorted. "Exactly as Tasha requested. White roses, sprays of lavender, and whatever Jacqui thinks will make it beautiful."

"Jacqui? As in Jacqui Livingston from high school?" Serena shoved her hand on her hip. "I suppose you've dated her, too."

"We went on a couple of dates a few years ago, Serena. She owed me a favor, so I got the flowers wholesale."

"What kind of favor?" Serena raised her brows.

"Hey, no worries." Justice sipped from the glass he held.

"Oh, when it comes to you, I worry," Serena stated. "Start talking."

"Jacqui, who is Jacqui Greene now, divorced her husband around the same time we got ours. She needed a job, so I helped her get into CTR."

"Computer Tech and Repairs. Where you work?"

"Yes." Justice met Serena's eyes. "Jealous?"

"No." Serena folded her arms. "You started dating while she worked at CTR, I take it."

"On and off for about a year. Nothing serious. Jacqui's dream was to open a flower shop. She had the perfect last name for it. Greene's Flower Shop. She worked hard, saved her money and two years ago her dream came true."

"I remember her talking about it at our tenth high school reunion." Serena paused. "Wait a minute. You've been in touch with her ever since, haven't you, Justice?" She punched his arm. "Why am I the last to know?"

"There's nothing to tell, baby. I love *you*," Justice replied.

"Love?"

"I meant loved."

"You have too many secrets, Justice Alfred Tate. I can't keep up."

"Hey, don't announce it to the world."

"What? Your secrets?" Confused, Serena stared at him, waiting for more information.

"My middle name. I go by Justice A. Tate. That's how the Harringtons know me."

"You're embarrassed of your middle name?" Serena huffed. "Your parents named you after your maternal grandfather." She fixed her gaze on Justice, hoping to make him uncomfortable. "It will come up eventually."

Justice eyed the surrounding area and whispered, "Keep it to yourself for now."

Get to the reason you wanted to speak with the man. "What time will Jacqui deliver the flowers tomorrow? I need to be here when they arrive. Also, did you know Tasha wants Jade to present her with the bridal bouquet?"

"Ten a.m. and yes." Justice set his glass on the bar and winked. "I guess I'll call it a night. See you tomorrow."

"You're not going anywhere," Jade said from behind Serena. "We need to talk."

Justice turned to his daughter. "Something wrong?"

"Yes. Tasha is all wrong for you, Dad. You shouldn't marry her. I hate her."

"Jade, keep your voice down," Serena said under her breath. "Everyone is looking."

"Let them," Jade grumbled. "If that woman tells me to do one more thing, I'll kill her."

"Jade, sweetie, you're overtired, and the wedding stress is getting to you." Serena grasped her daughter's upper arm. "Let's go home. Things will look better in the morning." She glared at Justice. "Tell your woman to back off our kids. And as you said, see you tomorrow."

Chapter Four

Serena entered the reception hall at ten a.m. to find a woman hovering over boxes of flowers. She had pulled her dark blonde hair into a high ponytail to keep it from falling in her face as she worked. Medium height and build, Serena recognized her at once. "Jacqui?"

The woman glanced up from the flowers, appearing irritated until she saw Serena. "Serena!" Jacqui extended her arms. "So good to see you again. It's been a long time."

"High school reunion," Serena said, giving her a quick hug. She stepped back and looked into Jacqui's hazel eyes. "Sorry to hear about your divorce."

"Ancient history." Jacqui waved a hand. "I'm sure you feel the same way."

"Going on seven years," Serena replied. "I moved on with my life."

"I heard." Jacqui continued to sort flowers. "He works at this hotel. Is that how you met?"

How much does she know? What has Justice told her? "Jack is a great guy," Serena said. "Can I help with anything?"

"I'm sorting the flowers for the centerpieces. I see the tables are set, and you have arranged the candles and vases on the tables. Those glass vases are understated but sophisticated. I bet they're designer pieces. Nice job."

Compliment Shari Harrington, not me. Although she tried, Serena had nothing to do with choosing the décor, yet she stayed silent. "I'll start pouring water into the vases."

"Not too much, Serena, and pour equal amounts."

"I'll try my best." Serena headed for the kitchen to find a water pitcher. When she returned, Jacqui had bouquets of flowers grouped and ready to go.

"Never mind," Jacqui said, taking the pitcher. "I'll do it myself. You know what they say. If you want something done right, do it yourself."

Should I be insulted? Serena checked the worktable. "Anything else I can do?"

"Yes. See that large white box?" Jacqui tilted her head in its direction. "Whatever you do, do not open it. It's the bridal bouquet."

"Does Tasha get the honor?" Serena asked.

"Per request. Please remind your daughter to keep the box closed. I wish I could show it to you. It's one of my best." Jacqui filled a vase and moved on to the next one.

"Has anyone told Jade not to open the box?" Serena sent off a text message to her daughter in case she didn't know. She then removed the box from the flower table and set it in a safe space. "I need to go home and change for the wedding," she said. "But if you still need me, I'll stay."

Jacqui stopped working and turned to Serena. "We didn't have time to catch up. Maybe at the reception?"

"Sounds good. You'll have to tell me about your flower shop and when you dated Justice." *Oops. That second part just slipped out.*

"He told you." Jacqui walked towards Serena. "It was never supposed to be a secret, but Justice likes to keep his personal life private."

"Yes, he does." Serena paused. "I found out last night."

"Oh. Sorry."

"Not a big deal, Jacqui. Justice said you dated on and off for about a year."

"Really?" Jacqui's hazel eyes lit up. "I thought we were a couple during that year."

"He probably didn't want to hurt my feelings, Jacqui, and made it sound more casual than it was."

Jacqui blinked a few times, and said, "I thought the relationship was going somewhere until I discovered he was seeing Tasha." She exhaled. "As friends, he said when I questioned him."

"Did you end it then?" Serena asked.

"I was hesitant, but yes, I did. It hurt because I loved him."

Not another one. "And now he's marrying Tasha. I'm surprised you're doing the flowers."

"You should talk. You're the event planner." Jacqui chuckled. "We're quite the pair, aren't we? Two exes helping the guy marry someone else."

"Yeah." Serena didn't want to explain how she got the role of wedding planner. "I'm going to head home. Don't forget the dress code. No red, black or white. Preferably shades of green, gold or lavender."

* * * *

Serena held up her dress and studied it. She had debated color and style for weeks. "Did I make the right choice?"

"You did." Robin poked her head into Serena's bedroom. "Teal is your color, darling. Do you need help with your dress? I just finished with the girls. We're ready when you are."

"I need one more minute. The photographer wants us to arrive two hours early. He'll do his best to get all the photos he can except for the bride and groom together." Serena gazed at her mom. "Did you ever think I'd go to Justice's wedding, let alone be his wedding planner?"

Robin let out a hearty laugh. "No, I did not see that coming. Hopefully, things will settle down after they are married." She tapped her chin. "Or will they?"

"Between you and me?" Serena lifted her brows. "Tasha likes drama. Even if she marries the man of her dreams, I can't see her changing."

"Then we better buckle up," Robin teased. "We'll wait downstairs for you. Don't take too long."

"Oh, and Mama?"

"Yes?" Robin turned to look at Serena.

"You look wonderful. Sea green was a great choice."

Serena waited until her mom closed the door. She sat on the edge of her bed and took a calming breath. "Please get me through the day. I will try to be the better person and not let Tasha's demands and nonsense affect me." She stood and straightened her dress. "There. Ready as I can be."

The girls' voices traveled up the stairway. "The limo has arrived," Jewel announced.

"Better let mom know," Jade said. "Mom?"

"I'm coming," Serena answered as she came down the stairs.

The ride to The Pearl felt different from Serena's usual daily trip. A quiet unease settled in her chest as they approached the hotel. Her senses sharpened, searching for what could be wrong. She shook her head to shrug off the feeling. *Today, things will be different. Nothing will go wrong.*

Serena told herself she was a guest at an exclusive wedding with over two hundred invited guests. Tasha's parents spared no expense. Following the ceremony, guests would receive the finest champagne to toast the couple. Servers would circle the room with caviar, along with other expensive hor d'oeuvres. Serena could see it all in her mind as they entered the hotel. *A perfect day.*

Shari Harrington greeted Serena's family at the bridal room entrance. "Good, you're here. I think that's everyone." She turned to the photographer. "You can start taking pictures of the women in Tasha's wedding party. Jade?" Shari took her hand and led her toward the other bridesmaids. "Once they finish with you, please get the wedding bouquet to present to Tasha."

"Sure." Jade gave her a smile, which Serena had seen before. *Jade's best fake smile. You go, girl.*

"I guess I'll join them, too," Jewel said, rolling her eyes.

"Shari didn't mean to overlook you, baby. She wanted to give Jade last-minute instructions," Serena replied, hoping to soothe Jewel's hurt feelings.

Serena helped the photographer to the best of her ability, trying to stay busy. Before Jade left to retrieve the flowers, she reminded her daughter not to open the bouquet box.

"Mom." Jade exhaled. "Everyone has made it clear that Tasha gets to open the box. Then the bridesmaids will pose with her and a thousand more photos will follow."

"You're holding up well, sweetie." Serena patted her arm.

"I'm tempted to open it before I come back to the room. She'd never know," Jade giggled.

"But I know you won't. Your mother raised you right." Serena stared at her. "Besides, I saw the box this morning. From what I remember, the florist used a decorative seal to close it. You would ruin the seal if you tried to open it."

Jade dropped her shoulders. "You spoiled all the fun."

"Don't make me send Grandma with you," Serena said in a teasing way. "Now go."

* * * *

The presentation of the flowers began as Jade walked slowly toward Tasha, who sat in a high-back winged chair. Jade placed the box on her lap and backed away, taking her place among the other bridesmaids. Everyone clapped as Tasha broke the seal and 'oohed' and 'aahed' over the flowers. She lifted the bouquet from the box and examined it. "They're just what I ordered…I mean, wished for." Tasha glared at the photographer. "I hope you got everything."

"Yes, I did," he nervously nodded. "Do you want me to proceed with the group shot?"

"Yes." Tasha turned her head and sneezed. "Oh, my goodness." She waved her hand in front of her face. "I have no idea where that came from."

Once the photographer finished, Tasha's mom gave an order. "Everyone out except for the bridal party. It's time."

"That includes you, Mother," Tasha said in a sarcastic voice.

"Of course." Shari adjusted the top of her strapless plum-colored mermaid dress.

After checking out Shari's attire, Serena felt bad for Justice's mom. She had tried to help her choose a dress and shoes for the wedding. "I can't compete," she had told Serena.

"Then don't," Serena had answered. "Just be your wonderful self."

Justice's mom, Gloria, had always been kind to Serena and treated her like a daughter. Since Justice severed ties with Serena, contact with his family had become more difficult, and she finally gave up. She missed only her mother-in-law from that time in her life. Over the past year, she encouraged the girls to get to know their grandmother. "She's an interesting woman," she had told them. Gloria appreciated the gesture and had reached out to Serena, wanting to include her in their adventures. *You look lovely in your appropriate dark green mother-of-the-groom dress, Gloria.*

Serena approached Tasha. "Do you want me to leave, too?"

"No." Tasha shook her head. "You have a job to do. Stay and line up the girls. Then you can leave."

Yes, your majesty. "Sure." Serena turned towards the women. "I believe Zuri is first?"

"Then me." Jewel got in line behind Zuri.

"And I follow Jewel," Jade said.

"Wait," Tasha called. "I've changed my mind. I want Jade to be my maid of honor."

"What?" Mandi's face turned a deep shade of red. "I've got that honor, Tasha. You can't take *that* away from me."

Serena gave Tasha a "What are you doing?" look.

"It's my wedding," Tasha replied. "I'm allowed to change my mind."

"Fine," Mandi huffed. "But after this wedding is over, our friendship ends."

"I'll be so busy being Mrs. Justice Tate, I won't notice," Tasha said.

"Girls. Women, I mean." Serena held her hand up like a stop sign. "Enough. It's an emotional day. You don't mean what you're saying. Work this out later."

Mandi slipped in front of Jade. "I'll be the bigger person. I wouldn't want to ruin Justice's day."

Serena looked at Tasha, who was inhaling the scent of her bouquet. "I'll lead them out." She turned to the women. "Take things nice and slow. Wait for about a minute before the next person steps onto the runway. Ready?" She opened the bridal room door and headed for the reception hall where she bumped into Mr. Harrington.

"Where's the bathroom?" he asked Serena.

Oh, dear. Serena pointed to the men's room and said, "Go straight to the bridal room afterward." She heard Zuri giggle and gave her a stern look.

"Come on, it's funny," Zuri said. "Tasha will have to explain she was late coming down the aisle because her dad was in the bathroom."

* * * *

Serena encouraged Zuri to smile as she ushered her to the white linen runway. It led to the outdoor gazebo where the wedding would take place. When Serena returned to the doorway, Jewel appeared at the correct moment.

"Don't worry. I've got this," Jewel whispered when she walked past her mom.

"Only two left, and hopefully, Theo Harrington is headed to the bridal suite," Serena said under her breath.

Jax, Justice's brother, had escorted Shari Harrington to her seat, then led the groomsmen to the gazebo where they now stood. Justice walked out and took his place next to his brother, hands folded in front of him. He showed no emotion, and his blank expression alarmed her. Something felt terribly wrong at that moment. The music sounded off-key, and people's faces looked distorted. Serena's stomach flipped over, and she squeezed her hands together. *It's nothing. Last-minute nerves. My job is almost done.*

"Serena," Mandi hissed, breaking into Serena's thoughts. "My dress. Could you check the back, please?"

Serena scooted around the woman and zipped the dress to the top. "Did you ask anyone to help you?"

"No." Mandi shook her head. "I can dress myself."

And you did a fine job. "You're good to go," Serena said, gesturing to the walkway.

Serena turned, expecting to see Jade, but no one stood in the doorway. She checked the time. "Knowing Jade, she wants to make the perfect entrance."

After another minute ticked by, Serena felt a prickling sensation go up her spine and across her neck. "Something's wrong," she mumbled. "I better go check."

Hurrying toward the bridal room, a rush of bad memories flooded Serena's mind. She saw Ava Taylor, supermodel, lying on the runway during Mia's fashion show last winter. Dead after drinking poisoned champagne. Someone stabbed Amber Morelli, a mobster's daughter, to death during a cheerleading reunion during the summer. Nina had discovered her body in a hotel hallway. Carmody Fletcher, almost killed by a wooden nutcracker during the holiday season. *No, this is a wedding. Nothing like that can happen.*

Serena threw open the door to find Jade standing over Tasha, who was still sitting in the Queen Anne's chair. Tasha's body was bent over the flower box, her head buried deep in the bouquet. "Jade? What's going on?"

"I think she fell asleep, Mom." Jade gave her a worried look and placed a hand on the back of Tasha's head.

"Oh, no! What's happened to my baby?" A voice came from behind Serena. "Take your hand off my daughter, Jade," Shari Harrington screamed. "You're suffocating her."

Chapter Five

"I did nothing." Jade's voice trembled, and she raised her hands in the air. "I was checking to see if Tasha fell asleep."

"Asleep?" Shari screeched. "Stand back. Let me look at her." She shook Tasha's shoulder. "Wake up." She checked around the room. "Is she drugged? What did you give her?" Her eyes met Serena's. "What did your daughter do to mine? Or are you in this together?"

"Jade would never hurt anyone, Shari. I suggest we call 9-1-1. *Immediately.*" Serena had not brought her phone and inwardly scolded herself. *I need to find Jack.* She looked at Shari. "Do you have your cell?"

"No." Shari threw out her hands. "I was in such a rush I left it at my seat. When I saw you run from the reception hall, I followed."

"Mine is in my purse." Jade gestured to a table. "I'll call."

Serena followed Jade and wrapped her hands around her daughter's shoulders. "You okay?"

"No," Jade whispered. "I think Tasha is dead."

A stinging sensation whipped through Serena's body. Her head spun with ways to help Jade and discover why this happened. "Send a text to Jack first," she said under her breath.

Shari was too busy tending to Tasha to notice what they were doing. She petted her daughter's head and said, "Help is coming, baby. Hang in there."

"Shari?" Theo's voice startled Serena. "What the hell is going on?"

"It's our baby, Theo. She won't wake up." Tears streamed down Shari's cheeks. "Do something."

Theo held up his phone. "I'll call for an ambulance."

"We already did," Serena said.

"I'll double-check, if you don't mind." Theo gave her a harsh look.

He doesn't believe me. Serena stared at Jade with wide eyes. "You called, right?"

"Yes, they should be here any minute."

"What about Jack? Have you heard from him?" Serena's voice shook.

"Not yet." Jade checked her phone. "You told him to work security and not attend the wedding. The office is in the basement, Mom. He'll be here." Her cell beeped. "It's him. Jack just got off the elevator."

"I'll go meet him and tell him what's going on," Serena said.

Serena headed for the bridal room door, but when she reached it, someone blocked her path.

"Hold on there, missy. You aren't going anywhere."

"Detective." Serena took a step back. "Bill Mitchell."

At one time, Jack and Detective Bill Mitchell worked together at the SFPD. Bill never liked Jack and made an unauthorized deal with him. If Jack resigned from the department, Bill would release a suspect Serena and Jack needed for leverage against the true supermodel killer. It had succeeded, and they got the confession, but Jack had to sacrifice one of his passions, detective work, to achieve it.

Despite Bill's hopes, solving the high-profile murder case never led to a promotion. Serena sensed he blamed her for interfering and costing him the advancement he believed he deserved. Now, whenever he discovered any issues at The Pearl, no matter how minor, he'd come to the hotel and start asking questions. Serena feared this wasn't a minor incident but a full-blown murder.

"That's right, Ms. Tate, it's me." Bill gave her an evil smile. "This time you won't interfere with my case because…" He waved his hand around the room. "You are a suspect." Bill nodded toward Jade. "And so is your daughter."

Serena stepped in front of Jade. "She did nothing wrong. If you want to point the blame at someone, choose me."

"Mom." Jade nudged her.

"Or both of them, officer," Shari yelled. "Don't let them get away. Theo talk to the police officer. Make sure he understands."

Although she was in dire straits, Serena held back a giggle. Bill hated when someone referred to him as an officer and always corrected them. "I'm a detective," he would say. Obviously, Bill knew the Harringtons and would refrain from correcting her.

Two paramedics wheeled a stretcher into the room. "Ma'am," one said. "Please step aside so we can examine the patient." He checked Tasha's pulse and looked into her eyes with a small light. Giving a slight shake of his head, the room understood its meaning. Tasha was dead.

"Seal off the reception hall," Bill Mitchell called over his shoulder to officers stationed at the door. "No one leaves until we interview every guest. Where's Sue? She should be here by now. Check her status."

Sue Downing headed up forensics and worked on other cases with Jack. Serena met her when she helped with the model murder case. She and Jack appeared close, and Serena had been a bit jealous. Since then, she learned Jack considered Sue a friend and valued her opinion. Serena breathed a sigh of relief, knowing Sue would be on the case.

Serena heard an argument coming from the hallway and inched closer to the door. *It's Jack.*

"I don't care what you say, Bill. I'm The Pearl's security chief, and I have authorization to enter the room."

"Fine. But stay away from your girlfriend," Bill growled.

The medics had lifted Tasha onto the stretcher as Bill entered the room. "Any preliminary guesses?' He stared at the men until one broke down.

"When I pulled the patient into a sitting position, I swear I smelled peanuts. Crazy, right?" He lifted his shoulder.

"Don't touch that bouquet," Sue Downing commanded from the doorway. She slipped on gloves and approached the chair. "Are you her mother?" she asked Shari.

"Yes." Shari could barely speak as she wept in her husband's arms.

"Give me a quick health history."

"Peanuts? She was highly allergic to them."

Jade met Serena's eyes. "Did Tasha go into anaphylaxis shock? Allergic reactions can cause it to happen. It makes it hard to breathe."

"You are correct," Serena whispered. "Your body goes into shock and if you don't get treatment…" She couldn't finish the sentence.

Serena turned towards Jack. She prayed he understood the look she conveyed as she slid her eyes toward Sue. *Find out what's going on.* He bobbed his head once and approached Sue.

"How can peanuts get into a bouquet?" Jack asked.

"Look carefully, Jack." Sue pointed to the petals. "See that light dusting? Someone shook peanut dust onto this bouquet." She addressed the room. "Who had access to this bouquet?"

"Jade." Shari pointed a shaky finger at Serena's daughter.

"What about the florist?" Serena snapped back. "In fact, anyone could have seen the box on the table and opened it." *Not with that seal, but I'll do anything to protect Jade and place the blame elsewhere.*

"Tasha wanted the box to remain closed and requested a special seal so no one could tamper with it," Theo said, patting his wife's back. "Jade was to deliver it, *unopened*, and place it on her lap. Obviously, the girl had other ideas. She discovered a way to open the box and apply the dust."

"Jade didn't like Tasha," Shari cried. "I heard her say at the rehearsal that she could kill her."

"That's just a saying," Serena replied. "Everyone says it and doesn't mean it."

"But Jade *did*," Shari snarled. She had gained her composure and was going on attack.

Serena gave Sue a pleading look. *Please do something.*

Sue gave a nod and said, "The medics took Tasha to the hospital, where they'll do a complete analysis. My team will transport any evidence we find to the station. Bill?" She turned to him. "Anything you want to add?"

"Yes. Pete? Ramona? Escort those two to the station's holding cell." Bill gestured to Serena and Jade. "Now."

"You can't do that, Bill," Jack said. "You have no proof of their guilt. It's all hearsay."

"The proof is there. We just need to find it." The short, heavy-set officer with tufts of brown hair on either side of his balding head made a disapproving noise as he rubbed his hand over his protruding stomach. "I believe Ms. Tate is just as guilty as her daughter. She probably forced the poor girl to do it. Jealousy makes you do strange things."

"What?" Serena took a step toward the detective, but Jade held her back. "You're making that up."

"Looks clear cut to me," Bill said smugly. "Jealous ex murders new wife."

"Before you take them away," Theo Harrington bellowed. "Find that no-good son-of-a-gun groom and lock him up, too. He probably helped them." He shook a finger at Serena and Jade.

"As you wish." Bill dipped his head and gestured to two of his officers. "You heard the man. Find Justice Tate."

Jack had managed to make his way over to Serena while Bill held court with Sue and Theo Harrington. "Do as the man says," he said under his breath. "Go along with everything. I will start an investigation as soon as I leave the room." He turned to Jade. "Don't offer any information, Jade. In fact, don't speak except to your mom. Got it?"

Jade, who appeared to be in shock, nodded her head vigorously. Serena wrapped an arm around her daughter's shoulders. "It will be alright. Think of who is in our corner, Jade. Jack, Nina, Mia and Lily."

"Even Gram," Jade murmured.

"And you've got me." Serena hugged her tighter.

"The police can only hold you for forty-eight hours," Jack said. "When the time is up, they must charge you or release you."

"Then you have forty-eight hours to prove we didn't do this, Jack," Serena replied. "If I can make a suggestion, find Jacqui Greene. She's the florist. And Justice. Start with them."

"Got it." Jack reached for Serena's hand and squeezed. "If I don't come to the station to see you…"

Serena gave him a weak smile. "I'll know why. You'd rather be catching the killer. I'd do the same thing." She stole a quick kiss. "I love you."

"And I love you forever," Jack whispered. He hugged her, then Jade. "Take care of each other."

"We will," Serena said as tears filled her eyes. "If I am charged, Jack, please tell me you'll go on with your life. Find someone…"

Jack held up his hand. "You're getting a little ahead of yourself, Serena. It won't come to that."

Serena folded her arms over her chest. "Promise."

"Okay. I promise." Jack rolled his eyes. "I've texted Nina, and she's meeting me in the hall. I need to slip out before Bill decides I should come to the station."

"Go. I trust all of you." Serena watched Jack move deftly to the entrance and out the door.

* * * *

"Sir." An officer stood in the bridal room doorway and cleared his throat. "We cannot locate Justice Tate. It seems he has left the building."

"What?" Bill's face turned a rich shade of purple. "Put an APB out on him immediately."

"Mom." Jade tugged on Serena's hand. "I've heard of APBs, but I always wondered what the letters stand for?"

"All-points bulletin," Serena answered. She wrinkled her brow. "Did they check the men's room? Kitchen? I don't understand why your father would run."

"Was Dad involved in Tasha's death?" Jade gasped and covered her mouth. "I was an innocent participant in his deadly plan."

"Jade." Serena closed one eye and tilted her head. "You've inherited my drama gene. Justice did not play a part in this. Trust me." *Then why did he run? Does Jack know? He needs to find Justice ASAP.*

"If you'll come with me," the woman police officer, who Bill had called Ramona, said. "I will not cuff you unless you resist."

"We won't," Serena answered. She and Jade followed the officer through the door. They passed by the reception hall, but the doors were closed. "I forgot to tell Jack to take care of Jewel," she cried.

"He will, Mom. Jack's our hero." Jade walked beside her mother, tall and proud. She'd found her courage.

Pleased that her daughter could hold her own, Serena slid her hand into Jade's. "I won't let them accuse you of this. If anyone goes down, it will be me."

* * * *

Hours slipped by and no one had come to visit them. Surprised they weren't being questioned, Serena snuggled against Jade, who had fallen asleep in her arms. She had fought Bill Mitchell when he wanted to put them in separate cells. "Jade stays with me!" Serena had yelled.

Sue Downing intervened, pulling Bill aside. After a lengthy conversation, he agreed. "Just until we get the facts," he grumbled.

Serena kissed the top of her daughter's head, recalling memories from when she was a baby. Feisty yet loving, Jade, the older of the twins, had entered the world screaming at the top of her lungs. When Jewel appeared, she blinked and gave her sister a questioning look as if to say, "What's going on with you?" They bonded from the moment they were born.

"They always remain your child," a voice beyond the bars declared.

"Nina!" Serena carefully laid Jade on the cot and rose to greet her. "What are you doing here?"

"I'm here to give you a ride home. The police have released you from custody."

"How?"

Nina stood silently with her lips pressed together.

"You *do* know the commissioner." Serena jabbed her pointer finger at her friend. "Am I right? Bill Mitchell swore you were close friends. He wanted you to speak to the man about promoting him."

"Sometimes I wish I had. He wouldn't be on this case."

"I like how you avoided the question, Nina," Serena said with a smile. "Is it true? Jade and I are free?"

"Yes," Nina answered. "For now."

"How is Jewel? I need to see her. Is she still at The Pearl?"

"No, Robin took her home. After the police questioned her and Robin, they let them leave, along with the others. They've informed the wedding guests they are to stay in the city until the police finish their investigation."

"Great, she'll be at home when we arrive. I need to get Jade into her own bed. When can we leave?"

"When they finish processing the paperwork. But you, Serena, won't be going home. You're coming with me. Robin is waiting to take Jade home."

"Why? Can I at least go home first?"

"We have no time to waste. We must head to the hotel. Jack needs your help."

"With what? Or should I say who?" Serena asked as everything began to make sense.

"Your ex-husband. He seems to have disappeared into thin air."

Chapter Six

Serena and Nina arrived at The Pearl Hotel after midnight. The usual hum of daily activity had died down to an unhurried and tranquil nighttime vibe. Jack waited by the red Torii gate, which led to the Japanese gardens.

When people walked into the main entrance of The Pearl Hotel, the gardens greeted them. Stepping through a red Torii gate, visitors would find an authentic Japanese setting. Serena's beloved pond and its stunning fountain sat in the center of the gardens. Many paths wound through the beautiful landscape, which ended in secluded cul-de-sacs or led people to various shops and restaurants. This magnificent setting helped The Pearl secure a place as one of San Francisco's top ten attractions.

Usually, the sight of the gardens made Serena's heart soar, but not tonight. She had a feeling of dread and couldn't shake it. Even Jack's warm embrace didn't help.

"Jack, you must do everything in your power to prove Jade is innocent. I don't want her accused of this crime," Serena whispered in his ear.

"You know I will, Serena." Jack hugged her tighter before letting her go. "But first things first. Let's go to the security offices where no one can hear us."

Serena furrowed her brow and lowered her eyelids. "I finally am invited to the bowels of the hotel to play double-oh-seven," she said in a sad voice. "I get to see where you disappear every day, but the thrill is gone. I'm so worried about my daughters, nothing would impress me."

"It's okay," Jack replied. "I understand, but I really need your help."

"I will be in my apartment," Nina said. "If you need me."

"You mean the penthouse?" Serena closed one eye.

"I'm glad you haven't totally lost your sense of humor, Serena." Nina patted her arm. "Remember, I'm only a phone call away."

"What about Lily and Mia?" Serena asked. "Did you update them?"

"Yes." Nina nodded. "We'll meet in the tearoom tomorrow. When it's convenient."

The trio walked to the elevators, and Nina used her keycard to open her personal cubical. Serena and Jack stood in silence while waiting for theirs to arrive. Once it did, Jack escorted her inside and said, "Tell me why you think Justice ran."

"Do you want a list?" Serena asked.

"I'm sure you made one during the ride to the hotel." Jack chuckled. "Sorry. This is serious."

"It's fine. Humor helps." Serena slipped her hand into Jack's. "Last night, Mia thought Justice did not look happy during the rehearsal dinner. Unlike a man ready to marry his true love."

"Was she?" Jack lifted a brow. "Tasha declared Justice was her love over and over, but he never responded in return."

"I don't know how Justice felt about Tasha. He said nothing to me." Serena shook her head. "When I spoke with him at the end of the evening, he was drunk. Not the happy or celebratory kind. It seemed like he was drowning his sorrows."

"Not the appropriate behavior for a man about to get married," Jack said.

"Justice insinuated that Tasha told him what to do, and he did it. For example, the flowers."

"And you've brought us right back to the key piece of evidence," Jack replied. "The bouquet."

"The fatal bouquet," Serena whispered. She gazed at Jack as fear crept up her spine. "It's just speculation, but wouldn't Justice need to approve the flowers before the florist sealed the box? He could have shaken peanut dust onto it when she wasn't looking."

"Let's discuss in my office." Jack gestured for Serena to exit the elevator. "This way, please."

The security area's design prioritized function and accessibility. Two or three monitors sat atop every workstation. Toward the back, a hallway led to additional offices.

Jack led Serena into the chief of security's office. A functional yet impressive mahogany desk occupied the center of the room, facing the entry. Decorators had positioned guest chairs in front of the desk. A leather couch and chairs for informal meetings filled the back of the room. Monitors hung on the walls along with detailed maps of the hotel.

"Jack!" Serena placed her hand on her heart. "This is not what I pictured."

"Not James Bondy enough for you?" Jack teased.

Serena had always kidded Jack that he was like James Bond, disappearing into a special room where new gadgets and equipment waited for him. She had coined the word, James Bondy.

"It's wonderful." Serena exhaled. "Now let's get to work."

"We usually work in your office, Serena," Jack stated. "We can go there once I show you what I've found. I know you want to start your murder board."

"I would like that." Serena nodded.

"We'll go…" Jack hesitated. "After you get some sleep."

"Sleeping seems impossible," Serena exclaimed, throwing out her hands.

"You need to rest your brain so you can think better," Jack said. "Please consider going to your room when we're done."

"Only if you come with me. You need to rest your brain, too." Serena raised her brows.

"How can I resist?" Jack kissed her and caressed her arm. "Shall we sit?" He pointed at the sofa. "Look at this monitor." Once they took their seats, Jack gestured to a large one opposite the sofa.

Serena glanced up to view the monitor hanging on the wall in front of her. Jack pressed a remote button, and the screen came to life.

"Here is a list of Tate surnames with reservations in the city or this hotel. Let's start with the first one. Joseph Tate."

"He is Justice's father. Gloria and Joseph are staying here at the hotel."

"James Tate." Jack highlighted the next name.

"Justice's uncle. Joe's brother. I believe he and his wife are also staying here."

"So far, it makes sense and checks out. The others are not hotel guests." Jack clicked to the next name. "Dwayne Tate."

"Justice's cousin and one of his groomsmen. He probably couldn't afford a room here, even at the reduced price for wedding guests."

"How about this one?" Jack asked. "Alfred Tate?"

An alarm went off inside Serena's head. "That's Gloria's father, but he passed away." She held up her pointer finger. "It's also Justice's middle name. His parents named him after his grandfather."

"Did he register under a false name?" Jack met Serena's eyes. "Justice knew the police would look for him, so he couldn't return home or leave the city. He couldn't produce a fake ID. Not in this day and age. Using his middle name grants him time."

"Check what credit card he used," Serena said.

"Already did. He paid cash."

"It's him," Serena stated. "Let's go surprise him." She rose from the sofa, excited they found Justice so quickly.

"It's two in the morning, Serena. Let's get some sleep, then head out in the morning."

"Okay. You win. This time." Serena took his hand. "We must keep Nina informed. I'm sure she's awake and waiting for answers."

"We'll text her in the elevator," Jack answered.

"I'll send one to Mia and Lily. I'll set up a tearoom meeting for lunch."

"You and your tearoom," Jack replied with a shake of the head. "Am I required to go?"

"No, you can resume your usual activities and do James Bondy things." Serena kissed his cheek. "But first, I want you all to myself."

* * * *

"Does the Tate family have a tradition of using the letter 'J' for names?" Jack asked, holding the door open for Serena.

"Yes," Serena answered. "Joe kept the tradition, but as you can tell, James did not."

"Dwayne." Jack nodded, then pointed at Serena. "Jade and Jewel. 'J' names."

"I didn't mind." Serena slid into the back of The Pearl's limo. "They are my most treasured gemstones. Justice wears a bracelet embedded with a jade and a diamond."

"Diamond for Jewel?"

"He said it's the most precious jewel."

"Clever."

The limo cruised through the city until it stopped at a simple chain hotel. Serena peered out the window, heart racing, hoping Justice was inside. They planned to catch him by surprise before he realized they found him. The driver parked and exited the car. He circled the front and opened the back passenger door for Serena and Jack. "I'll wait here," he assured them.

Jack walked up to the desk, flashed a badge, and said, "I need Alfred Tate's room number."

"Um." The desk clerk bit into his bottom lip. "I need to check with the manager."

"Fine. Tell him Nina Takeda will wait for his phone call."

"The Pearl hotel's Nina Takeda?" the man asked in a shaky voice.

"Yes, that's the one." Jack bobbed his head. "Well? Make the call."

The desk clerk turned his back as he spoke on the phone. "Yes, sir. Immediately, sir." He faced Jack and Serena. "Room three-ten."

"Do not warn him." Jack stared daggers at the man.

"I won't." He held up his hands in surrender.

"Where are the stairs?" Serena asked.

The desk clerk gestured to a door. "There."

"Jack, I'll text you when I reach the third floor. You watch the elevator until then." Serena headed for the stairs. "I'll get my cardio for the day," she said under her breath.

Serena texted Jack when she stepped into the third-floor hallway and waited for his arrival. Checking the door numbers, the first one said three hundred one. The stairwell door opened, and Jack smiled at her. "All clear. Let's see if Justice is home."

* * * *

"Open up, Justice. We know you're in there." Serena pounded on the door. Silence greeted her. "Come to the door. Our children need you." She faced Jack and widened her eyes. "What should we do?"

"Justice, it's Jack," he called. "They've arrested Jade for Tasha's murder. We need to talk."

"They didn't arrest her," Serena whispered, then realized what Jack was doing. "That's right, Justice," she shouted at the door. "Do you want Jade to sit in jail for something she didn't do? We need your help."

The door moved, and Serena held her breath. It barely opened as Justice said in a dejected voice, "Come in."

Serena shoved the door back and entered the room. Justice still wore his wedding suit, although the tie was missing and the shirt unbuttoned. His eyes looked red and puffy after Serena got a closer look. She noticed a bottle of whiskey sitting on the small table by the window. It was half empty. He'd bought the pint size, yet she couldn't believe he could sit in a hotel and drink.

"Why did you leave The Pearl?" Serena asked. "The police needed your statement."

"I panicked," Justice replied, sinking into a chair by the table. "I knew I would be the first person the police would suspect. Plus." He hung his head. "Theo Harrington could prove I had a motive."

Serena gasped. "Something felt wrong when Theo directed Bill Mitchell to find you."

"Please, take a seat." Justice gestured to the other chair by the table.

Jack took the chair, and Serena sat on the edge of the bed. "Start talking, Alfred, and it better be good."

"Huh." Justice lifted his shoulders. "I should have known you'd figure it out, Serena. I hoped using my middle name would buy me some time, but you located me quickly."

"We don't care what name you used, Justice. Be glad we found you, and not the police." Serena used a sharp tone. "Tell us why Harrington could provide the police with a motive."

"First, I want to say." Justice reached for her hand. "I had no idea the police arrested Jade. I'm sorry."

"The police took us both to the station for questioning," Serena said. "I'm a suspect, too."

"What?" Justice widened his eyes. "You said they arrested Jade for the crime."

"We may have embellished the truth." Serena slid her eyes toward Jack.

"We needed you to open the door, Justice," Jack said. "I'll do whatever it takes to protect Serena and the girls."

"And I'm not?" Justice inhaled and sat straighter in his seat.

"You want the truth?" Jack asked in a stern voice. "No. You put yourself first when you ran from the hotel."

"You're hoping I'm guilty, don't you, Security Guy?" Justice asked, balling his hands into fists. He slammed one against the table. "Then you can have my family all to yourself."

"Like you ever cared about family," Jack shot back.

"Gentlemen." Serena placed her palms on the table. "Let's refocus and return to the reason we're here." She turned to Justice and grabbed his arm. Tapping the bracelet, she said, "Do this for them. You are going to tell us what Harrington has on you."

"Fine," Justice huffed. "I never wanted to marry Tasha." He looked out the window and continued speaking. "When she discovered I was divorced, she texted me. Don't ask how she got my number or knew about the divorce."

"I'm sure one of your many girlfriends gave her the information," Serena replied in a sarcastic voice.

"Serena," Jack said. "You're not helping."

"Sorry. Go ahead, Justice."

Justice faced Serena. "Tasha wanted to reconnect and reminisce about old times. It was easy. I already knew her and felt comfortable, so I agreed to meet her. Plus, whenever we got together, she paid for everything. It was an enjoyable time. I never thought she considered me her boyfriend."

"How did Harrington get involved?" Jack asked.

"Last September, I got a call from him. Theo asked me to come to his office. He had a proposition for me. After we met, I said I'd consider it."

"What was it? Money?" Serena asked.

"No, something better." Justice shook his head. "I never should have agreed to it. I have job security, a recent promotion and a good salary. I got greedy."

"What did he propose?" Jack asked, leaning toward Justice.

"Theo Harrington is a prosperous lawyer and has invested his money wisely. He owns a real estate firm and promised to make me CEO of the company if I'd marry his daughter. The salary was five times what I make now. He gave me until the end of the year to decide. I proposed to Tasha on New Year's Eve."

"So, you don't love her?" Serena kept her anger in check. "You've strung Tasha along for seven years, Justice. Her father makes an offer you can't refuse, so you finally ask her to marry you." She shook her head. "You'll never change."

"I did it for the girls, Serena." Justice threw out his hands, tears filling his eyes. "What can I say?"

"I can't tell you what to say," Jack replied. "But I know you're in a heap of trouble."

Chapter Seven

"Tasha died before I could marry her," Justice yelled. "Doesn't that make me innocent? Someone else did it."

"A lawyer could argue you hoped the allergic reaction would occur after the ceremony. Unable to see Tasha prior to the wedding, the bouquet was your only option," Jack answered. "He'd say you used too much peanut dust or you didn't expect Tasha to keep smelling the flowers before the wedding."

"What makes you an expert?" Justice smirked.

"Jack's here to help you, Justice," Serena answered in a stern voice. "If you don't want it, we'll leave."

Justice wrinkled his brow. "How can Security Guy help?"

"First off, stop calling him Security Guy and use his real name," Serena responded. "*Jack* is more than a security guard at The Pearl. I keep trying to tell you that. He's head of the division. Previously, he worked for Mr. Takeda in LA after serving time in the military."

"Okay, whatever. If you can help me, Jack, what's the next step?" Justice stared across the table at Jack, then his gaze went to Serena. "Well?"

"You must go to the police station and turn yourself in," Serena answered. "But not before Jack instructs you on proper behavior, and we get more answers from you."

"Right now, you're the grieving groom," Jack said. "You fled the hotel when you heard Tasha died. You needed space and weren't thinking clearly." He let out a breath. "Do you have a contract with Harrington? Anything in writing? Or is it his word against yours?"

Serena's heart skipped a beat, fearing the answer. "Justice, you must have signed a contract," she said. "Theo Harrington is a lawyer. It wouldn't be a handshake or just giving his word."

"We did. It's locked in a safe in his office," Justice announced. "There is no way we can get to it."

"I didn't mean for us to steal it," Jack said with a sigh. "But I need to know everything."

"*Okay.* We don't need to steal his," Justice replied. "I have a copy."

"Why didn't you lead with that?" Serena asked. "Having a copy might help your case. Jack and I always start our investigations with means, motive and opportunity. You have the means and a motive. We need to focus on opportunity. Did you visit the floral shop to approve the bouquet or choose the flowers?" *This is an important question. If he went there, I don't think we can prove he's innocent. Or maybe he isn't.*

"No, I never went to the shop."

"Are you telling the truth?" Serena narrowed her eyes. "This was your one and only task for the wedding. Surely you must have seen the flowers."

"I did."

"Could you please be more specific?" Serena asked, trying not to sound annoyed.

"I texted Jacqui for help, and she promised to put together the perfect bouquet if I sent her a list of flowers," Justice answered. "When she finished, she said I could stop by anytime to see if they met my expectations. Since I didn't care, I said I was busy with last-minute tasks. I asked her to send a picture and gave final approval via text."

"Do you still have the conversation and photo on your cell?" Jack asked.

"Of course."

"I can get a copy of Jacqui's texts," Jack said.

"You can?" Justice lifted his brows.

"He can," Serena stated and beamed with pride at Jack. "Jacqui is also your alibi, Justice. We need her to tell the police you never came to the floral shop."

* * * *

"I just thought of something. Jacqui is also *my* alibi," Serena said as she and Jack left the hotel with Justice in tow. "I never went to the floral shop either."

"You and Jacqui were alone in the reception hall the morning of the wedding," Jack stated. "They could still use that against you."

"Jacqui had already sealed the bouquet in the box. She made a big deal about no peeking or trying to open the container. It sat on a table next to a pile of flowers Jacqui was sorting, so I moved it to a safe place."

"While you were together, did Jacqui ever leave the reception hall?"

"No, only me. I got water from the kitchen to fill the vases. Jacqui never left the hall."

"It might be enough to clear you," Jack said.

"What about my daughter? How will it help her?" Justice climbed into the limo after Serena and Jack.

"By speaking with Jacqui." Jack answered. "She might become our star witness. You texted her, right?" he asked, gazing at Justice.

"She hasn't answered yet." Justice held up his phone. "But she will."

Within ten minutes, Jacqui answered, and Jack gave directions to the driver. They discussed ways Jacqui could assist on the way to her condo. Serena hoped she might help Jade, too.

Jacqui answered the door with her dark blonde hair flowing around her shoulders. Serena thought she looked younger and less business-like than their meeting at the reception hall.

Jacqui appeared upset yet gave them a smile. "Come in. I made tea and coffee." She patted Justice's arm. "You look like someone who could use a strong cup of coffee, my man."

Justice covered Jacqui's hand with his own. "Thanks."

Jacqui's condo was modest in size, with a living room furnished with a couch and two chairs. Serena sat on the sofa, positioned between the two men.

Once they settled in, and Jacqui poured the tea and coffee, she asked, "How can I help?"

"Justice said he never came to your shop to approve the flowers. Is he correct?" Serena longed for her journal— one she never went without when writing her novels. She hadn't given it a second thought until now.

"Yes." Jacqui nodded. "We did the order through texts. I can show you my cell phone."

"You don't need to, Jacqui," Justice said, jabbing his thumb at Jack. "This guy already has it."

"What?" Jacqui widened her eyes.

Serena elbowed Justice in his ribs. "What Justice meant is that Jack has the ability to request the records."

"Oh." Jacqui sipped her coffee and smiled at Serena over the cup. "I'm still willing to show you the texts."

"If you don't mind," Jack said in a kind voice, holding out his hand. After he examined the phone, he asked, "Could you walk us through the day you designed the wedding bouquet? Was the shop busy? Did anyone from the bridal party stop by to chat?"

"I've told the police everything," Jacqui answered. "I spent the morning at the station."

"They won't share the report with us," Jack answered.

Serena wiggled in her seat. "Jacqui, would you please retell what happened prior to the wedding?" She gave her a pleading look. "My daughter's life depends on it."

"Let me start by saying neither you nor Jade came to my shop before the wedding," Jacqui stated. "The bride requested I seal the box shut at the shop. She wanted no one to see it before her. If someone tried to open it, Tasha could tell. I placed a special foil seal on the box. You would have to slice through it with your nail or something sharp to open it. You couldn't peel it off and reattach it. If you removed it, the seal would not stick to anything again."

"I saw the box when Jade brought it to the bridal room. The seal was still intact," Serena whispered. "That clears her."

"And you," Jack said in a quiet tone, then shifted his gaze to Jacqui. "Did you speak with Detective Mitchell, Jacqui?"

"Yes, he didn't seem happy that I gave you an alibi, Serena," Jacqui chuckled. "I hope I helped."

"You did more than help, Jacqui. Thank you." Serena hopped from her seat to hug the woman.

"We've got to stick together, right?" Jacqui winked. "Call me anytime if you need me, Serena."

Serena returned to her seat and pointed at Justice. "What did Bill Mitchell say about him?"

"I could only read his expressions. He didn't confide in me, Serena. But after I showed him the texts, Mitchell exited the room. I believe he made a phone call. When he returned, he continued the same line of questioning."

Jacqui sighed. "I'm sorry, Justice. I think you're still on his list."

"Theo Harrington wants me to pay for this," Justice replied. He massaged the spot between his eyes. "But I'd rather be a suspect than Jade. I'm okay with it."

"Jacqui, do you have pen and paper?" Serena asked.

Jacqui wrinkled her brow at the strange request.

"She likes to write things down," Jack said.

"Oh." Jacqui nodded. "I read an article about you, Serena. As an author, you always carry a notebook with you so you can jot down ideas. Will you turn this into your next story?"

"No." Serena shook her head. "I wasn't thinking of my book, but I'd still like the pen and paper."

"Of course."

After Jacqui delivered the supplies, Serena asked, "Are you willing to provide names? People who came into your shop?"

Jacqui locked eyes with Justice. "I've already told the police, so I guess you should know. Your mom, Justice. She came to the shop twice. One visit occurred the day before the wedding while I was prepping the flowers."

"What?" Justice looked stunned. "She never told me."

"Gloria said you'd never come to approve the bridal bouquet, so she did the next best thing. Checked for herself."

Serena wrote Gloria's name on the notepad Jacqui had given her. "Anyone else?" she asked.

"Shari Harrington." Jacqui rolled her eyes. "I swear she visited every day leading up to the wedding. Mandi and Zuri visited on Thursday, but Zuri left ahead of Mandi. Mandi stayed to talk privately with me. The shop was busy that week. Lots of weddings. Flowers sent to hospitals. People even placed orders for Father's Day."

"Did Mandi stay until you closed up the shop so you could speak without customers?" Serena asked.

"No, she needed to get to the rehearsal. Zuri and Mandi waited for me in the back of the shop. Whenever I got a break, I went back for a quick visit. We chatted about the wedding flowers and my business. After Zuri left, I found a few minutes to speak with Mandi."

"What did you discuss?" Jack asked.

"We talked mostly about the wedding. Mandi felt Justice was making a big mistake marrying Tasha. She acted quite possessive for a woman who had a crush on him in eighth grade." Jacqui rolled her eyes. "That was so long ago. Apparently, she hasn't gotten over you, Justice."

Serena nudged Justice. "Care to defend yourself?"

"I didn't know she liked me. I was thirteen." Justice slumped against the couch cushion. "No matter what I say, I look guilty."

"Then you better start talking," Jack said. "I told you I need to know everything."

"Okay." Justice blew through his lips. "I dated Mandi after I stopped seeing Jacqui."

"You forgot Tasha." Jacqui snorted. "*He* strung her along for years." She looked at Serena as she directed a finger at Justice. "Mandi never knew why I broke up with Justice. I told her about Tasha the day she visited the shop. She was shocked."

"What about Zuri?" Serena asked. "Did she know Justice saw Tasha even if he dated someone else?"

"Yes. Zuri appears to know everything," Jacqui smirked. "But, she always forgives whatever Justice does."

"Would you like to add anything?" Jack faced Justice.

"Zuri and I slept together the night before the wedding." Justice hung his head. "She came to my place. I was drunk."

"Enough." Serena held up her hand. "I've heard enough. I get it. You were sleeping with Zuri, Mandi and Tasha during these last couple of years."

"Maybe? But not at the same time." Justice peeked at her. "Only when I wasn't seeing the others."

"Oh, yes, of course. That makes it better." Serena jotted the names on her notepad. "Keep going, Jacqui. There's more, I bet."

"This one will surprise you," Jacqui said. "Evan Peterson."

"Which one is he?" Jack turned to Serena.

"The white guy in the bridal party," Serena answered. "He played high school basketball with Justice and Jarrett. They were inseparable. Still are."

"Why would Evan poison the bouquet?" Justice asked. "He didn't have the means. Or motive. Especially motive." He glanced at Serena. "Isn't that what you use to judge if someone is a suspect?"

"Yes." Serena nodded. "You listened quite well."

"Maybe I can help. Did you put Evan in charge of the men's boutonnieres?" Jacqui directed her question at Justice.

"I gave him the job. The more I could delegate, the more I did. I never told him to pick them up at the shop, though. That was his decision. On the day of the wedding, Evan was supposed to locate the boutonnieres and make sure the guys pinned them on their suits."

"He was quite interested in the color and the proper way to attach them to the lapels," Jacqui replied. "As I took hold of his shirt, Evan asked if we could use the back room. I got the feeling he was uncomfortable with my staff and customers watching."

"Jacqui." Justice folded his arms. "Evan was making his move. I think he likes you."

"Maybe." Jacqui lifted her shoulder. "He visited a few times last week."

"Did he ever ask you out?" Serena widened her eyes.

"We went for coffee." Jacqui appeared flustered, as if she'd said too much. Her cheeks reddened, and she avoided Serena's gaze.

"We've overstayed our welcome," Jack said, placing his coffee mug on the tray. "Thanks for the coffee and the information, Jacqui. I think we've got all we need." He stood and turned to Justice and Serena. "Shall we?"

The sudden change in the conversation gave Serena a start. She followed Jack's directive, knowing he had a reason. They said polite goodbyes and headed out the door to the limo sitting in the driveway, waiting for their return.

Once inside, Serena stared at Jack and said, "Why did we leave? It was just getting good. Jacqui was about to tell us about her date with Evan."

"Was she? I think she was done talking." Jack raised his brows. "It's a discussion for another day, Serena. You and Jacqui at the tearoom."

Chapter Eight

"The tearoom is the perfect place to chat," Serena said. "Great idea, Jack. I'll invite Jacqui to tea and have her meet me at The Pearl." *Time to send a P.I.C. message to Lily and Mia and bring them up to date. I need to shorten my suspect list and begin to eliminate people.*

The limo pulled into The Pearl's driveway and stopped at its main entrance. Justice tapped Serena and gestured to the driver. "Could he take me to my place?" he asked. "I'd like to shower and change."

"I'll give you an hour, Justice," Serena answered. "Then call Bill Mitchell and turn yourself in."

Justice shuddered. "I don't like the sound of that."

"Jack is going to contact him and pass along the recent evidence. That should help your case."

"Jack knows Bill Mitchell?" Justice wrinkled his brow.

"Do you ever pay attention, Justice Tate?" Serena huffed. "Jack worked as a detective at the station until… Never mind. Yes, Jack knows Bill, and they have history. Be careful what you say. Only answer Bill's questions. Do not volunteer any information or say Jack is helping you. Got it?"

"Got it. Thanks, babe." Justice kissed her cheek.

"Justice!" Serena swiped at her cheek and slid from the passenger's seat, hoping Jack hadn't seen. "Jack, please inform the driver to take Justice home, then wait to take him to the police station? If Justice tries anything funny, he is to call you."

"Okay." Jack leaned into the open car window to speak with the driver. He patted the door, joined Serena on the sidewalk, and they watched the limo drive away.

"He better stick to his promise," Serena said, more to herself than Jack.

"Don't be so hard on him, Serena. He may not have loved Tasha, but he lost his fiancée today."

Serena stopped just inside the lobby. "You're defending Justice?"

"Yeah." Jack tilted his head toward the gardens. "Why don't we visit your favorite place and continue our conversation there?"

"With Sam? I haven't seen or talked to him in ages," Serena said, rushing to the entrance.

Serena recalled her first encounter with the fish. Nina had filled the pond with beautiful koi of every color, yet one fish stood out. A majestic red koi with white fins and tail. He'd emerge whenever Serena visited and appeared to listen to her problems. When she discovered she could communicate with him, Serena was thrilled. She had to ask yes or no questions, but Sam understood. He'd swim underwater and pop up his head for "yes" answers, and his tail for "no". She'd named him Samurai for his strength and loyalty.

"He won't appear if I come with you," Jack said. "But once we're done, I'll leave so you can talk."

"I don't understand why Sam won't meet you," Serena answered. "I plan to find out whenever I get a peaceful moment."

"There haven't been too many of those." Jack chuckled. "Tell him I'd like to know why, too."

The couple headed down the flagstone path, taking them through The Pearl's lovely Japanese gardens and approached the white bench placed across from the pond. Jack waited for Serena to sit, then sat beside her, placing his arm around her shoulders.

"You may not like what I'm about to say," Jack grimaced. "I feel sorry for Justice. He's stuck in the past."

"What do you mean?" Serena asked, wrinkling her nose. "Justice has obviously lived a full life since our divorce."

"Think about it, Serena. The man has only dated women from his high school years. *Your* high school years. Maybe he hoped you'd get jealous since you know the women."

"An excellent observation, Jack, but I don't see the connection. Besides, I had no idea he dated them until now."

"True. Was Justice popular in high school?"

"Yes." Serena nodded.

"The girls loved him, and then he started dating you," Jack said. "It's a safe place to go, Serena. He's going back to simpler times."

"When you put it that way…" Serena patted Jack's knee. "You're a good man, Jack Ando. Thanks for helping Justice. He doesn't deserve it after the way he's treated you."

"Are you referring to when he calls me Security Guy?" Jack laughed. "It's better he thinks that's all I am."

"You're that, and so much more." Serena checked the surrounding area before giving Jack a long, lingering kiss. "I love you."

"I love you forever," Jack whispered. "And am reluctant to leave you, but I must start some background checks. May I see your list of suspects?"

Serena dug in her purse and unfolded the paper. "Here. Take it."

"Just hold it up. I'll snap a picture. I assume you want to start your murder board after meeting Lily and Mia?"

"You know me well."

"Keep in touch, babe." Jack had left the gardens before the realization hit Serena.

He called me babe. Jack, you are dropping your guard and enjoying life. Serena chuckled.

A red koi sprung from the water. "Looks like a certain fish agrees." Serena walked to the white Japanese-style railing which surrounded the pond and leaned against it. "Hey, Sam. With the wedding preparations taking up much of my time, I've ignored you. Sorry. But, I'm here now."

Serena told Samurai what happened on Friday, and his mouth opened and shut whenever she reached an unsettling part of the story. "Jack and I have just returned from questioning the florist. This is the beginning of our investigation." She liked the sound of that. Serena and Jack were a team. "Now that I've updated you, I have an unrelated question." Serena inhaled. "Do you like Jack?"

The red koi dove deep into the water, and Serena wondered if he'd ever return. She noticed a few bubbles, and Sam's head appeared. "You like him! Why won't you meet him?" She paused. "Sorry. That isn't a yes/no question. What should I ask?" Serena tapped her chin. "Will you ever meet him?"

Sam swam in a circle and popped up his head. "Great!" Serena's phone buzzed. She checked the screen and saw Mia's name. "Ooh, I've got to go. Mia and Lily are waiting."

* * * *

Mia and Lily, engrossed in a conversation, never noticed Serena entered the tearoom. Serena approached the table, cleared her throat and waited.

"Serena!" Lily hopped from her seat and embraced Serena. "I'm so happy they let you out of jail. Trust me. I know what it's like."

"Very true." Serena nodded, recalling that Lily had to once prove her innocence, too. "I've got proof that will exonerate Jade and me."

"We heard about Jacqui Greene's visit to the police station. Maybe Jade will go free, but not you," Mia said, peeking over Lily's shoulder. "I'm so sorry, Serena." A tear trickled down her cheek as she hugged Serena. "Please, sit. We ordered your favorites—almond cookies and oolong."

"Thanks," Serena said in a shaky voice. Her heart pounded as she asked, "Why am I still a suspect?" She took a calming breath. "You heard that Jacqui Greene spoke with the police this morning? I was never at her floral shop." She reached for a cookie, hoping it would help her nerves, but today it tasted like sandpaper.

"Grandmother only got you a reprieve, Serena," Mia answered. "Bill Mitchell insisted you stay on their suspect list, no matter what evidence he received. According to him, Jacqui's testimony cleared Jade, but not you. You were alone with Jacqui and the flowers in the reception hall. We've got forty-eight hours to produce fresh evidence."

"Are you alright, Serena?" Lily covered Serena's hand with hers.

"No…I mean, I will be." Serena stirred a teaspoon of sugar into her tea. "Why is Bill Mitchell out to get me? I did nothing to him."

"Except solve his cases," Lily replied. "He blames you for not getting that illusive promotion."

"That's on him," Serena said in a bitter tone. "I'd love to file a complaint against him, but it would only make matters worse."

"We rechecked guests' movements on the day of the wedding," Mia responded. "Searching for any missed clues."

"I've done some research of my own," Lily said. "Nina spoke with Sue Downing this morning and passed along the information to us. Test results showed the killer sprinkled peanut butter powder on the flowers. One can easily buy it in stores. Anyone could have purchased the powder and had it ready to use."

"That makes it hard to eliminate anyone." Serena sighed. She produced the list Jacqui had given her. "These are the Thursday shop visitors, prior to the rehearsal. Jacqui always arranges flowers in the back room and that is where she'd keep the wedding items."

"Justice's mom is on the list." Mia widened her eyes. "How well do you know her, Serena?"

"Quite well. She'd never harm anyone."

"It makes sense that Shari Harrington would visit the shop. Even Zuri and Mandi," Mia said.

"Ooh, let me tell you something I learned about Zuri." Serena lowered her voice. "She slept with Justice the night before the wedding."

"What?" Lily slapped her hand on the table. "She had a motive to sprinkle the bouquet with the powder. The person responsible never intended for this to end in murder. They just wanted to stop the ceremony."

"And hoped Justice would come to his senses," Serena said. "Makes sense." She locked eyes with her friends. "Zuri goes on my murder board."

"Absolutely," Lily replied. "I don't like saying this, but you must put them all on for now, Serena. Even Gloria."

Serena hung her head. "You are correct, Lily. I can't ignore the fact that my ex-mother-in-law might have something to do with the crime."

"What about Mandi?" Does she have a reason to sabotage the bridal bouquet?" Mia asked.

"I believe so, but I need to speak with her privately. There's more to her story." Serena sent a text to Mandi, inviting her to lunch. "I'll be at the tearoom all day tomorrow. I've invited Jacqui for breakfast and Mandi to lunch."

"Who is this person?" Mia tapped the paper. "Evan Peterson."

"He's one of Justice's friends from high school. Justice thinks he likes Jacqui, and the wedding gave him an excuse to visit the shop."

"Did he ask her out? It would help his case," Lily said.

"Jacqui said they went for coffee. I'll find out more from her tomorrow."

"An excellent start to the case," a voice behind Serena declared.

"Nina, how do you do that?" Serena asked, placing her hand over her heart.

"Do what, my child?"

"Appear out of nowhere." Serena smiled at how Nina always called her "my child" and made her feel like family. Over the past two years, they had supported each other through difficult times and celebrated joyful occasions.

Now, more than ever, she needed Nina's encouragement and support.

"I was right there." Nina gestured over her shoulder. "Perhaps you didn't see me." She took her seat at the table. "I am sorry about Detective Mitchell, Serena. He is a stubborn man but is in charge of the case."

"He made sure he was, I bet," Serena mumbled.

"Nothing we can do about it," Nina replied. "Except move forward. Lily." She turned to her. "I'd like you to stay with the peanut butter powder aspect. Think of ways you would apply it without being seen. Research which stores carry it." She paused. "Serena, when you meet Jacqui tomorrow, ask if she noticed any substance on the petals before she closed the box. Mia and I will speak with Gloria. I can't imagine why she would interfere with her son's wedding."

"Maybe if he told her the real reason, she might," Serena said.

Three pairs of eyes locked onto hers.

"Go on," Mia said.

"Theo Harrington made Justice an offer he couldn't refuse," Serena replied. "Nothing sinister. Not like a crime boss would," she clarified. "Theo promised to appoint Justice CEO of his real estate company if he would marry Tasha."

"Wow." Lily wrapped her hands around her teacup. "It's also Justice's alibi. Why would he kill Tasha before the ceremony?"

"Hopefully, Justice is at the station now. I encouraged him to tell the truth," Serena said. "Jacqui said he never came to the shop, and their texts prove it. It won't take long to clear him."

"He still may have done it," Lily replied. "How close are Justice and Evan? I can see Justice asking Evan for a favor. He could have said, 'Sprinkle this on the bouquet when you visit Jacqui. Just enough to make Tasha sick so it stops the wedding.'"

"A good scenario, Lily, but they'd postpone and marry another day," Nina said. She held up her pointer finger. "Perhaps Evan thought of it all on his own. He wanted to help his friend and never thought of the consequences."

"But," Mia interjected. "Does he know Tasha had a peanut allergy? I find it hard to believe."

"True," Serena said. "It almost rules him out." She wrapped a few cookies in her napkin. "If you'll excuse me, I'll take these with me to my office and start my board."

"I'll have a pot of tea sent to you," Nina replied. "Anything else?"

"Yes." Serena nodded. "Start thinking of means, motive and opportunity for each person on the list. You know where I'll be."

Chapter Nine

"This is a lovely tearoom," Jacqui exclaimed. "Thanks for inviting me, Serena. I needed this." She placed a hand on her heart. "This flower scandal has hurt my business. Can you believe I've had five orders cancelled, and it's only been two days since it happened?"

"Word travels fast these days," Serena said. "Plus, it was a high-profile wedding. Being a prominent lawyer in the city, many people know Theo Harrington. His daughter's wedding plans were all over social media. Tasha posted most of the photos and gained a lot of followers. Everyone loves a wedding."

"She tagged my shop in those pictures. It wouldn't take long for someone to think I was responsible. I'm already getting hateful comments on my business page."

"I'm sorry, Jacqui. How can I help?" Serena asked.

"Tell anyone who asks, I had nothing to do with the murder. I'm an innocent victim."

"I think it's time for tea. You need a distraction." Serena waved at Jun.

"Are you ready to order, Serena?' Jun asked when she arrived at the table. "We have a variety of croissants today. Would you like to start with a sampler plate?"

"That sounds wonderful, Jun. Yes, please bring a plate, but we'd like to order tea first."

"Your usual?" Jun winked.

Serena pretended to be annoyed. "I may want something else."

"Fine." Jun folded her arms and stared at Serena. "Tell me your order."

"Oolong." Serena hung her head. "You know me too well, Jun."

"Oolong is a fine tea, Serena. It's your favorite. Nothing wrong with ordering it all the time." Jun turned to Jacqui. "What would you like?"

"I've never been to a tearoom before," Jacqui replied. "The list of teas is extensive. I can't decide."

"Then let me help." Jun pointed to the menu. "Would you prefer a black or herbal tea? They come in many flavors, as does our green tea."

"Don't forget matcha and rooibos," Serena added.

"Stop." Jacqui giggled and held up her hand. "Jun, you pick for me."

"How does Angel's Dream sound? It's a mix of black and green tea flavored with maple and blackberry."

"Wonderful." Jacqui handed Jun the tea menu. "I can't wait to try the croissants."

Jun returned with two teapots and poured them tea. "Would you like your order now?" She asked Serena.

"Give us some time to enjoy our tea, Jun." Serena smiled at her, knowing Jun got the message.

Once they prepared their tea and took their first sips, Serena asked, "How is it?"

"Delightful. I'm amazed by the tea's flavor."

"Then you've been missing out," Serena said, pausing a moment to stir hers. "Jacqui, do you mind if I ask you a few questions?"

"About what?"

"Let's start with high school. You and Mandi were on the cheerleading team, but were you close friends? What can you tell me about her?"

"Well…" Jacqui gazed at Serena over her teacup. "You and I know she was part of Tasha's click. What did we call them?" She chuckled. "Tasha's court. The queen and her ladies-in-waiting. I couldn't put Tasha above all else, so I never tried to befriend her. I liked Mandi when she wasn't with them. We were casual friends and hung out sometimes. Boy, she liked to talk. I learned a lot."

Serena's phone buzzed, and she saw Jack had sent a message. "Meet me in your office after breakfast. Important."

"Is everything alright, Serena?"

"Just my boyfriend." Serena lifted her shoulder.

"Ooh, I want to know more about him. Spill." Jacqui leaned forward, appearing eager to listen.

Serena didn't want to discuss Jack, but it could lead to a conversation about Evan. She'd get back to Mandi later. "You met him."

"I did?"

"At your house."

"The Asian guy?" Jacqui lifted her brows. "He's smoking hot."

"Thanks...I think." Serena smiled. "Don't get any ideas."

"I won't." Jacqui glanced down at the table. "I may have found someone, too."

"Evan?"

"Maybe?" Jacqui's eyes twinkled. "I haven't seen him since our twentieth high school reunion, which, by the way, you didn't attend."

"I wasn't in the mood to discuss my divorce," Serena said.

"Understandable. Evan and I had that in common. We sat in a corner and poured our hearts out over drinks."

"I'm sorry. Were you both hurt badly?"

"Not really." Jacqui shook her head. "We commiserated over what losers we were."

"You weren't...aren't," Serena said. "Look at you. After your divorce, you got a successful job and invested the money into your shop."

"With Ryan's help," Jacqui said.

"Your ex?"

"Yep. He wanted a quick divorce, and I gave it to him. No alimony. No spousal support. I warned him one day I would come calling, and when I did, he better have my payment ready. I got it in writing as part of the settlement.

Ryan would give me a certain lump sum five years after we parted."

"Wow." Serena stared at her. "Good for you. See, you're not a loser."

"I tried to convince Evan of that, too. He visited me at the shop, and as I told you, we went out for coffee. He believes he did something wrong in his marriage and wants to avoid making the same mistakes."

"Is this the start of a relationship?" Serena asked.

"Probably not. Evan's a nice guy but…"

"No fireworks. I get it." Serena felt bad for the guy. *He likes her, and she doesn't feel the same.*

"There is, but he doesn't live in town. He's over an hour away. I can't see it lasting, especially since I put in a lot of hours at the shop," Jacqui said. "Enough about him." She exhaled. "We were discussing Mandi."

"Were you aware she liked Justice since middle school?" Serena asked.

"Did Mandi get you to fall for her sad tale of unrequited love for Justice since eighth grade? Such hogwash. Mandi watched and waited for him to break up with every girlfriend he had, then she'd swoop in, making herself available." Jacqui paused. "If you know what I mean." She arched her brow.

"What?" Serena stared into her cup. *I need to sort through this. Do I want to know about Justice's love life and conquests?*

"She is not as innocent as she looks, Serena. She flashes those big, baby blue eyes, and you think she's so sweet," Jacqui stated.

"Are you saying she may have sprinkled peanut dust on the flowers?" Serena inhaled and slowly released it. "You left her alone in the back room, didn't you? You had started the wedding bouquet, and it was easily accessible."

"You're right. I assisted customers out front, leaving Mandi alone in my workshop. I never thought I needed to guard the flowers. I'm not accusing anyone, Serena," Jacqui said. "I'm providing you with enough information to clear your name."

"Thanks," Serena said. "I appreciate it."

Jun arrived with the plate of croissants, and the women made small talk while they ate. After Serena finished, she said, "I need to go, Jacqui. But before I do, I want to ask you one more question. Did you know Zuri had slept with Justice the night before the wedding?"

"No, it was news to me." Jacqui widened her eyes. "When Justice revealed he'd slept with her, I almost fell off my chair." Her expression said it all. She didn't know about Zuri until yesterday, but Serena bet Mandi did. It sparked Friday night's fight. Zuri bragged about sleeping with Justice and announced she would see him that night. Perhaps she wasn't giving Zuri's motive enough attention, yet she needed to get to her office and speak with Jack.

"Breakfast is on me. Please stay and enjoy the tearoom." Serena stood and smiled at Jacqui. "It was great catching up. I hope we can do it again soon."

* * * *

Serena entered her office to find Jack waiting. Her gaze swept over the room, freshly redecorated by her daughters. She recalled a memory from last summer when she brought Jack, Jade and Jewel into her office to discuss revisions. The scene replayed in her head.

"Mom, are you ready?" Jade asked. "We've chosen a color scheme."

"I can't wait to hear."

"Navy blue walls, more like a dark blue, with white trim. A long light-oak desk will take the place of those counters and your smaller desk, along with a white chair of your choosing. Although we suggest a padded swivel one like this." Jade held up her phone.

Serena squinted to see. "Okay, I like it."

"Matching oak floating shelves on that wall," Jewel pointed to the right of Serena's desk. "And a brushed gold lamp on your desk. We'll work on decorating the shelves later. Photos of us are a must," she teased.

"You forgot the brushed gold geometric hanging lamp, Jewel," Jade reminded her, pointing at the ceiling.

"Sounds like I've got my work cut out for me." Jack chuckled. "We should paint first."

"And order these items," Jade added. "Mom, this is going to be fun."

"Flooring! Can we redo it, Jack?" Jewel asked.

Serena had beautiful chestnut hardwood floors. Examining the flooring, she said, "It would be a shame to remove this beautiful wood."

"We can sand and re-stain them," Jack replied. "Or I have a better idea. Keep them and cover them with a large rug."

"We'll find a cool one that you won't trip over, Mom," Jade said.

Serena chuckled at the memory.

"What's so funny?" Jack asked, swiveling from side to side in Serena's chair.

"I was remembering the day the girls shared their decorating ideas," Serena answered. "It feels like so much has happened since then."

"I'm about to add to that list," Jack said. "I checked in with Sue at the station to see if she had any updates. Let's sit." Jack got up and led Serena to the navy and white canopy-striped sofa on the far wall.

"Sounds serious, Jack."

"I believe it is." Jack shook his head. "Bill instructed the lab to send all test results directly to him. For his eyes only. Sue hasn't discovered a way to see them."

"Knowing Sue, she will," Serena replied.

"They've dusted the flower box and bouquet handle for prints," Jack said. "Those results could help Bill immensely."

"Us, too, Jack." Serena pressed her lips together. "He's doing this on purpose. Bill is so desperate to solve the case before us, he's making a huge mistake."

"I agree," Jack said. "It takes a team to solve a case. Not one man."

"Sue is our only hope, Jack."

"Like in that first *Star Wars* movie?" Jack teased. "When the princess asks for one person's help?"

"Yes, because Bill is determined to prove I killed Tasha even though I didn't. No one will help me except Sue. She is my only hope."

"Don't worry. If I know Sue, she's working on a way to see those results." Jack took her hand. "How was breakfast with Jacqui?"

"I kept it casual but learned that Evan asked Jacqui out for coffee so his interest appears real. Mandi is not telling the truth about Justice. It's more than an eighth-grade crush. And Jacqui thinks you are smoking hot."

"What?" Jack laughed and placed his hand on his heart. "Where did that come from?"

"Don't act so surprised, Jack. First, you *are* smoking hot, and second, I told her to find her own man, which led us to Evan."

"So, you should thank me," Jack smirked. "For being smoking hot. It helped in the investigation."

"I swear if I say or hear smoking hot one more time…"

Before she finished, Serena felt Jack's lips on hers. She melted into his arms and wished she could stay in his protective arms forever. Her phone buzzed, interrupting their moment.

"A text?" Jack asked.

"I should check," Serena said, searching for her handbag.

Serena had placed her purse on the floor next to her. After retrieving her phone, she announced, "It's from Mia. She and Nina visited Gloria at home."

"Would you read it aloud?" Jack raised his brows. "I'd like to hear."

Serena glanced at the screen, and her heart dropped into her stomach. "Grandmother and I drove to Gloria's house to speak with her. She agreed to answer questions and was eager to help, but she must stay on the suspect list. Gloria knew about Theo's and Justice's deal and wasn't happy about it."

Serena covered her face with her hand. Her mind raced, and she felt sick.

"Serena," Jack said. "Are you okay?"

"No, Jack, I'm not." Tears welled in Serena's eyes. "I wanted to remove Gloria from the list, not keep her picture on my murder board."

"Just because she knew, doesn't mean she did anything," Jack replied.

"Oh, you don't know her, Jack. She's like me. A mother bear who will protect her cubs at any cost. Stopping the wedding would be one way to do it."

Chapter Ten

Serena's fingers trembled as she dialed Gloria's number. "Come on. Pick up." She tapped her foot and stared at Jack with wide eyes.

"She'll answer," Jack said, placing a hand on her knee. "Stay calm. You mustn't upset her."

"Hello? Is that you, Serena?" Gloria answered the phone after five rings.

"Yes, they released me Friday night, Gloria. I need to speak with you."

"About the wedding?" Gloria asked. "I already told your friends what I knew." She paused. "How did they know about Justice's deal with Theo Harrington?"

"From me. I asked them to find out if Justice had confided in you," Serena answered. "I called to give you some advice. Do *not* tell the police about Justice's deal. Theo Harrington may have already given his statement, but I hope he left that part out. He doesn't want that kind of publicity. If Theo believes only he and Justice are aware of the deal, he won't accuse anyone else of his daughter's murder."

"Oh, my. I never thought of it like that." For a moment, Serena thought Gloria hung up, but then she said, "You don't think I…?"

"Not for a minute. It's the reason I called you." *But you're still on my suspect list.* "The police may want to question you again once they receive more information or evidence. Stay strong, Gloria. I plan to solve this mystery soon." *I've got less than forty-eight hours or back to jail I go.*

"Justice told me about your amateur sleuthing. If anyone can solve this, it's you, Serena."

"Thanks, Gloria," Serena said. "Can you do me a favor?"

"Sure. Anything."

"Contact me if you need to talk or have any ideas that would help our case." *Whoops. I just said 'our', like in hers and mine.*

"I will. Sending positive vibes your way."

After the call ended, Serena faced Jack. "What do you think?"

"You were factual and gave helpful advice," Jack said. He checked his watch. "Don't you have a lunch date with Mandi?"

"I forgot." Serena tapped her forehead. "Thanks for reminding me. But first." She rose from the sofa, walked to her murder board and removed the scarf which covered it. "This needs further review."

"Hey, you put yourself on the board." Jack gestured to her photo. "I must say you are thorough."

"I won't take my photo down until I'm sure Bill Mitchell has cleared me."

"He won't, Serena," Jack stated. "Think about it. He had the perfect excuse to lock you up so you couldn't investigate the case."

"You're right." Serena placed a finger on her cheek. "If Nina hadn't intervened, I'd still be there. I bet Bill's blood is boiling."

"Agree." Jack chuckled. "And it's the reason he's kept Sue from seeing any test results." He inched closer to the board. "I don't see Jade's picture up there," he said. "But it's okay, Serena. Sue assured me Jade is off Bill's list."

"Good. At least Sue knew that. Which leaves Gloria, Shari, Mandi, Zuri and Evan."

"Aren't you forgetting someone?" Jack asked.

"Jacqui." Serena folded her arms. "How did I miss her?"

"You've got a lot on your mind. Let's print her photo before you leave." Jack headed to Serena's desk.

Someone knocked on Serena's door as Jack passed by it. He opened it and said, "Lily, please come in."

"I'm glad you are still here." Lily smiled at Serena. "I'm up to my ears in peanut butter powder."

"Found anything?" Serena asked.

"I'm close. With our connections, it won't take long. I've requested lists from every store in the surrounding area that sells peanut butter powder, asking to see their inventory for the week of the wedding. I should receive their findings later today. Then Jack." Lily faced him. "You need to help me get security footage from the stores that sold the powder. It may be a long process, but I believe the killer purchased it this week. Not too many people keep it on their shelves."

"I'm ready to help," Jack said.

"I hope you're right, Lily." Serena hugged her. "You and Jack stay here and plan. I've got a lunch date."

"I wish you luck," Lily said, returning the hug. "We'll meet later and compare notes."

* * * *

"Serena," Mandi said. "It surprised me when I got your text. I thought you were in jail."

"They didn't have enough evidence to hold me," Serena lied, guiding Mandi to the Takeda table. "I wanted to speak with you about the wedding. Get your opinion."

"That detective." Mandi wrinkled her nose. "Interviewed me *twice*. Both times, Theo Harrington sat in during the questioning. Tasha's dad is out for revenge, Serena. If he had his way, he would ask the police to arrest all of us."

"He's a powerful man, so be careful," Serena said. "Do you get along with him?"

"I thought I did until this happened." Mandi rolled her eyes. "Theo feels both anger and grief. Tasha was his only child."

"Theo?" Serena raised her brows.

"He was Mr. Harrington until after college. Theo pointed out that I was an adult, and I should call him Theo. Don't make a big deal out of it, Serena."

"I'm just asking," Serena said. "I heard you visited Jacqui the day of the rehearsal."

"So?"

"She's told the police you waited for her in the back room…alone."

"I was with Zuri."

"Until she left."

"Are you accusing me of hurting my best friend?" Mandi touched her throat. "I'd never."

"Can you prove it?" Serena closed one eye.

"No." Mandi hung her head. "Look, Serena, I'll share a secret with you, and I hope I can trust you. You're aware I had a child during my marriage. She's everything to me. After the divorce, I struggled. Tasha helped me any way she could. Even financially. Why would I want her dead?"

"To get her out of the way. You might finally achieve your eighth-grade wish. Justice would become your boyfriend," Serena grimaced.

"Ha." Mandi shook her head. "Why would you think I want Justice?"

Do I tell her what Jacqui said and betray her confidence? I must. This is an investigation. "Jacqui said you hung around Justice, hoping he would break up with his girlfriend, but when he did, you never took her place."

"Really? Or is Jacqui jealous?" Mandi tilted her head to one side. "Let me tell you something, Serena. I dated Justice and broke up with *him*."

"When?"

"After Jacqui. She found out he was seeing Tasha and ended things. Justice turned to me for support. That's when…"

"You slept with him and promised not to hurt him, unlike those other women," Serena said in a sarcastic tone. "But something happened. You ended things, too."

"Between listening to his sad stories about you, and Tasha texting and calling him all the time, it got old. I love the guy, but he's too much."

"Yes, he is." Serena giggled, and Mandi joined her. Serena sat straighter and became serious. "You still didn't answer what happened at the flower shop."

"Nothing." Mandi exhaled loudly. "I keep trying to tell everyone that. If I had seen anything resembling peanut butter powder by the flowers, I would have discarded it. I told you why I would never hurt Tasha."

"Tasha was your ATM."

"Friend, Serena," Mandi huffed.

"Then you need to tell Detective Mitchell what you told me," Serena said.

"I can't."

"He'll keep you on the suspect list," Serena replied.

"Let him. I know I didn't do it," Mandi said. "Have you spoken with Zuri? That act of hers has limits." She fluttered her lashes. "She loves and cares about us all.

Zuri lives in another world where she and Justice are star-crossed lovers."

"So, you know."

"That she planned to go to Justice's room after the rehearsal dinner? Yes. She thought she could talk some sense into him." Mandi's lips curled into a snarling frown. "She probably slept with him, too."

"She did," Serena mumbled.

"What?" Mandi slapped the table. "I wondered why she seemed surprised the wedding was still on. Did Zuri think one night with her would change his mind?"

"If this isn't a soap opera, it should be," Serena said.

"What would you name it, Ms. Author?" Mandi chuckled.

"Let's not go there." Serena held up her hand. *I don't think Mandi tried to kill Tasha. The more we talk, the more I feel she's telling the truth. I need to schedule a P.I.C. meeting ASAP.*

"You write mystery or thriller novels," Mandi said. "I get it. You want to protect your idea." She arched a brow. "Justice says you enjoy detective work, too. That's what you're doing now, isn't it?"

"In a way, yes."

"Then meet with Zuri. Get her talking. I think she's hiding something," Mandi replied.

"I will. Thanks for the advice." Serena realized they hadn't ordered, except for tea. "Mandi, I'm sorry. I must go. Please stay and order anything you like on me. Jun will take care of you."

"I need to leave, too. My little girl is staying with my parents until this is over. I should check in with them." Mandi stood, slung her purse over her shoulder and said, "It was good connecting with you again, Serena. Too bad it was under these circumstances." She bent down and placed a kiss on Serena's cheek. "I hope you solve this quickly. Theo is in such pain, I'm afraid to see what he might do."

Serena stared at the tearoom wall, trying to process what she had learned. She hardly noticed when two familiar figures took their seats at the table. A warm hand covered her.

"Serena," Mia said. "We're here. I know you're overwhelmed, but the clock is ticking. Tell us what you learned."

When Serena completed the breakfast with Jacqui and lunch with Mandi stories, Lily said, "Gosh, everyone sounds guilty. I understand why you are confused, but this might help. I just received the stores' inventories. Five of them sold the powder last week. Jack is working on getting the security footage from them."

"It helps," Serena answered. "But I could be on the footage. I stopped at a grocery store to pick up a few items last week. I doubt if they place cameras in every aisle."

"No, they don't," Lily said. "Let's hope you didn't go in one that sold peanut butter powder."

"Is Bill Mitchell doing the same thing?" Serena asked.

"Perhaps." Lily lifted her shoulder. "He may have assigned people to check stores in the area. It could take longer if the police visit each store personally. We have better connections." She winked.

"I'd like to discuss Jacqui and Mandi now," Mia said. "They don't appear to have done it, but you should keep everyone on the list until we can positively rule them out. Jacqui owns the shop, which makes her accountable, but would she ruin her reputation and all she worked for to kill someone? I doubt it. Mandi has a daughter, so why would she commit murder? Besides, it sounds like Tasha was still giving her money. It makes no sense for Mandi to eliminate her."

"I feel the same way," Serena replied.

"Then get Zuri to the tearoom." Lily gestured to Serena's phone. "Tell her you ordered afternoon tea, and she should meet you here. I'll let Jun know."

"I'm on it." Serena sent off the text and hoped Zuri would respond soon. She hadn't left the tearoom all day except to meet Jack in her office, but didn't mind staying. "While we wait, I must call Mama and check on the girls."

"We should leave, so Zuri doesn't see us," Mia said. "We'll move to that table." She pointed across the room. "Grandmother plans to join us."

"I'll order afternoon tea for two tables," Lily said. "I haven't eaten since breakfast." She grinned at her friends. "It's great to be solving crimes again with my two best friends. We've got this."

* * * *

"Serena, is something wrong?" Zuri rushed to the table.

"If asking someone to join me for afternoon tea is wrong, then yes." Serena gestured to the chair opposite her. "Please, sit."

"I'm sorry if I'm overreacting," Zuri said. "For the last few days, stress has consumed me. How are you staying so calm? That detective arrested you on Friday."

"Look at me now." Serena held her hands out. "I'm not in jail."

Zuri took her seat and said, "If the police let you go, they don't believe you did it. I'm happy for you."

If only you knew. "Thanks."

"And Jade?"

"Is cleared." Serena noticed Jun coming with a tray of food.

"Oh, I'm sorry," Jun said. "I thought Lily said pronto." She smiled and winced at the same time.

"It's fine, Jun." Serena turned to Zuri. "Would you like some tea?"

"I'll have water," Zuri answered.

Jun set the tiered tray of finger sandwiches on the table. "I'll come back with your tea, Serena."

Serena had had her tea limit for the day. "Water sounds great, Jun." She studied the three-tiered tray. Her favorite cucumber sandwiches filled the tower, along with rare roast beef with horseradish cream and watercress. Egg salad on small croissants completed the choices.

The chef had placed whole fresh strawberries among the sandwiches. "Help yourself," she said to Zuri.

Once Jun delivered the ice water in two crystal goblets, Serena decided to enjoy the meal. She knew more food would come—scones with lemon curd and clotted cream followed by a tray of desserts. *Plenty of time to speak with Zuri about the wedding. I'll make small talk first, then build up to the big stuff.*

"I suppose you want to talk about the wedding," Zuri said, as if reading Serena's mind. "I can't stop thinking about what happened."

"Only if you want to discuss it," Serena replied.

"If you want my opinion, Mandi did it."

"Well, she thinks you did."

"Why that…" Zuri covered her mouth. "I won't say it." She smiled, but it didn't reach her eyes. "She envies my relationship with Justice. He confides in me."

"But not her," Serena clarified.

"Correct. Justice told me weeks before the big day he didn't want to marry Tasha."

"Then why did he?" Serena stared at Zuri, already knowing the answer. She had to discover what Zuri knew, so she acted clueless.

"I can't say. He's free now, so let's leave it that way."

"Perhaps you should tell me what you know. Your silence might cause the police to arrest an innocent person for Tasha's murder." Serena studied the woman. *How did Zuri discover Justice has an alibi? How close are they? He didn't call her with the news…or did he?*

"You can't tell the police, Serena. They'll arrest Justice if you do."

"I won't run to the police with the information, but hopefully, it will help my investigation."

Zuri nodded. "I heard you liked to do a little detective work from Justice." She hesitated. "Justice signed a contract with Theo Harrington. If he married Tasha, Harrington would make Justice CEO of his billionaire-dollar real estate company. See what I mean? It makes Justice look guilty as hell."

Chapter Eleven

"Justice Tate," Serena yelled into her phone. "Drop everything you're doing and meet me in my office *now*."

Serena cut short her meeting with Zuri, feigning a family emergency. *This qualified.* She paced from one end of her office to the other, sending texts to Mia, Lily and Jack while she waited.

Half an hour had passed, and Serena opened her phone to send Justice a text. She had called him to make sure he would get the message, but Justice may have chosen to avoid her.

"Serena?" Justice appeared in the doorway, gasping for breath. "What's so urgent? Are the girls okay?"

"Finally! Sit." Serena pointed to a chair next to the sofa. She sat on the couch and faced him. "The girls are fine." She gave him a stern look. "How many people did you tell about this contract between you and Theo Harrington?"

"I told you and Jack." Justice hung his head. "And a few others."

"Well, it's coming back to bite you now." Serena gave him a death stare. "If Bill Mitchell learns of this contract, he'll go after your mother. And Zuri. Am I leaving anyone else out?"

"Jax," Justice answered. "But I told him at the rehearsal dinner."

"You're certain that is everyone?" Serena closed one eye.

"Yes."

"I understand why you would confide in your mom and even Jax, but Zuri?"

"I could always talk to her, Serena. She is smart and gives excellent advice. We've been friends since middle school."

"Even during our marriage?" Serena asked in an accusing voice.

"Of course not. After our divorce, I made connections with old friends again. Zuri was one of them."

Serena recalled her earlier conversation with Jack. *You may not like what I'm about to say. I feel sorry for Justice. He's stuck in the past.* "Did you ever date her?" She crossed her fingers, hoping he'd say no.

"Yeah, but I like her better as a friend. I may have messed up things because we dated for a month. Within weeks marriage became a topic, so I had to tell her how I felt."

"You gave her the 'let's be friends' speech?"

"Yeah." Justice looked away, unable to make eye contact. "I hurt her feelings, but she eventually forgave me."

Darn. Zuri stays on the list. Maybe Justice can help me eliminate someone else. "What about Mandi?" Serena asked. "You dated her, too. Does she know about the contract?"

"Gosh, no." Justice shook his head. "She has enough reasons to hate Tasha without me adding to her problems."

"What? I don't understand. Mandi and Tasha were best friends. She told me Tasha helped her financially after her divorce."

"That's news to me," Justice replied. "Tasha always talked about how well Mandi was doing after her divorce, especially since she only worked part time. That's when their friendship fell apart. From what I recall, Tasha never gave her one cent."

"That makes no sense." Serena shook her head. "Mandi said Tasha has always supported her, especially after the divorce. Tasha chose her as the maid of honor."

"True. For the past year, Mandi has tried to repair the relationship. Don't ask me, Serena. Sometimes I don't understand women."

Serena made a mental note of the new information, then asked, "Is there more?"

"Yes. Theo contacted me. Although he'd like to see me go down for the crime, he realized I didn't do it. Bill Mitchell told him I had an airtight alibi. He warned me to keep the deal we made between us. No need for anyone else to find out since I'd never become CEO."

"Except for me, Jack, your mom, Jax and Zuri."

"Theo has no connection to them, Serena. He will never contact my family or Zuri. Besides, they won't say anything."

"I hope you're right, Justice. Zuri wasn't too happy you still went through with the wedding. What if she tells Bill Mitchell about the contract to get even?"

"Why would she?" Justice met Serena's eyes, appearing clueless.

"To put you back on the detective's radar. He would tear your alibi apart, looking for any mistakes. Bill is desperate to solve this case."

"We're friends, Serena. Zuri would never do that."

"Are you familiar with the 'woman scorned' quote?" Serena narrowed her eyes.

"Hell hath no fury like a woman scorned," Justice whispered.

"You need to take a hard look at yourself, Justice," Serena said. "Or don't date women who know one another." She could tell Justice had enough, so she said, "I should go home and see Mama and the girls."

"No, Serena, you shouldn't. I'll go. You only have one more day to clear your name." Justice took her hand. "Find out who did this, Serena. Tasha didn't deserve to die this way."

"If it makes you feel any better, I believe the killer didn't want Tasha to die. They just wanted to stop the wedding."

"Stopping the wedding wouldn't have mattered. Tasha would have chosen another day or dragged me to the courthouse to get married."

"Perhaps." Serena lifted her shoulder. "Then again, you might have chosen not to marry her or it would have given someone time to intervene."

* * * *

After Justice left, Serena leaned against the couch and stared at the ceiling. She needed to rest her brain, if only for a moment. The silence felt like a warm blanket, wrapping her in a calming hug. Her eyes fluttered shut, and she hoped to doze off, even for a few minutes. *Maybe I'll dream of the answer.*

"It's no use. I can't sleep, nap or doze until I solve this." Serena hopped off the sofa and stood in front of her board. "Something is missing." She tapped her chin. "Or someone." She walked to her desk. "Who wanted to stop the wedding? Once I have the answer, I'll solve the case."

"Hey, Serena," Jack appeared in the open doorway. "Can we talk?"

"Sure, but first I need a hug." Serena turned toward him and melted into his strong arms. She sniffed his shoulder. "No fair. You showered."

Jack threw back his head and let out a glorious laugh. "I'm glad you're still you, Serena."

Serena stepped back and placed her palms on Jack's cheeks. "I love you. You make things better." She kissed him, then pointed at her board. "Help me."

"I can do more than that. Lily and I finished watching security footage from five stores. We can mark the people who went shopping."

"And eliminate the rest?"

"No," Jack answered. "They might have already owned the powder and didn't need to buy it."

"Jack, that's counterproductive! My head is spinning. We must take someone off the board. I'm getting nowhere." Serena stared at the photos. "I was going to take Mandi down, but Justice changed my mind." She quickly told Jack about the conflicting stories. "Why would Mandi lie?"

"She's covering for someone," Jack replied. "Doesn't make her guilty, though."

"Please tell me some good news. Who went shopping?"

"Everyone up there except Zuri. Even you, Serena." Jack pressed his lips together. "Sorry. It won't take long before Bill receives this information and calls people to the station."

"Good. Maybe he needs to get us all in one room and start asking questions."

Jack grimaced. "Not yet."

"But you agree?" Serena lifted her brows.

"You want me to say you're right, don't you?" Jack smiled. "As I just said, not yet. We need to look at each suspect and start our game of means, motive and opportunity."

"So, it's a game?" Serena nudged him. "You always said to approach this seriously. Facts are our friend."

"Perhaps I used the wrong word…"

"Nope. I like it." Serena slipped her arm through Jack's. "Let's start with Shari Harrington."

"She had the means," Jack said. "In fact, they all did. Means refers to the tools, skills and methods to commit a crime. The tool was peanut butter powder. Easily accessible at any grocery store. It doesn't take much skill to sprinkle it on flowers."

"No one needed a disguise or an excuse to be around the flowers. This was a wedding," Serena replied.

"Right. So, on to motive. Shari may not have wanted her daughter to marry Justice," Jack stated.

"I don't blame her. If someone messed with Jade or Jewel for over twenty years, I wouldn't approve of their marriage to him. Who knows what he'd do in the future?"

"As you said, the suspects had many opportunities to dust the powder on the bouquet." Jack nodded. "Jacqui confirmed that people on our list came and went the day of the rehearsal. She had begun to arrange the flowers in her workshop, leaving the area to wait on customers. Those flowers sat unattended for hours. Our focus should be motive."

Serena tapped Jacqui's picture. "She's been too cooperative. We need to take a closer look at Jacqui. She dated Justice but discovered he was seeing Tasha behind her back. Perhaps she wanted revenge, or at the very least, disrupt the wedding."

"I'd like to take a harder look at Evan Peterson," Jack added. "I can't think of a reason he'd want to kill Tasha, but you never know. We may have missed something. Why don't we ask them to meet for drinks tonight in the hotel bar?"

"I like how you think, Mr. Ando," Serena said. "Two birds. One stone."

"If that's how you'd like to think of it." Jack turned his hand over, showing his palm. "Hopefully, you can take their photos down after our date."

"First, we need to extend the invitation." Serena tilted her head. "I believe Evan is still at the hotel. He wanted to avoid the hour drive into town if he was called in for questioning."

"He is in room four-twelve," Jack said.

"That was quick." Serena chuckled.

"Well, after all, I'm Security Guy." Jack chuckled. "I know how to get things done."

* * * *

"Jacqui is the obvious choice for our number one murder suspect, Jack. Why have we overlooked her?" Serena asked after they chose a table in the bar. "We should have immediately suspected her. Former girlfriend holds a grudge. Her ex marries the woman he was seeing behind her back. Jacqui, being the florist, had personal access to the bouquet."

"Did she know Tasha had a peanut allergy?" Jack tapped the table. "That's what we need to discover." He tilted his head toward the bar's entrance. "We'll discover the answer soon."

"Serena." Jacqui bent down to hug her. "It was so nice of you to invite us."

"Serena." Evan nodded at her. "Jacqui's right. Tasha's murder was awful, but it made us realize that time is short. Jacqui and I decided to continue our relationship and see where it leads." He gestured at Jacqui, then pointed to his chest. "I assume you knew."

"I'm happy for you," Serena said. "Please, join us."

An hour ticked by, and Serena engaged the couple in light conservation, even bringing up their high school years. She glanced at Jack and said, "It's been a long day."

"Definitely." Jack agreed. "It's been fun getting to know your friends, Serena." He gave Evan and Jacqui a solemn look. "Serena has had little sleep. I bet you can guess why."

Serena smiled at him as she finished her drink. *I love you, Jack. Great way to open dialogue about the case.*

"Tasha's murder," Jacqui whispered. She covered Serena's hand with her own. "I said I'd help any way I can."

"Perhaps there is a way," Jack said.

"Ask me anything," Jacqui replied.

"The dust on the flowers," Jack responded. "Did you know what it was?"

"Not until the detective told me." Jacqui wrinkled her nose. "Peanut butter powder? How strange."

"It was peanut butter powder." Jack dipped his head. "Harmless, unless you're allergic to it."

"I didn't know Tasha had a peanut allergy until Detective Mitchell told me."

"You've known Tasha since high school, Jacqui," Serena said. "You never heard about it?"

"Never. As I told you, Serena. I wasn't close to Tasha. Only Mandi. I didn't want to be part of Tasha's inner circle. Too much work."

"I remember," she answered. Serena almost believed her, but she ruled no one out without concrete proof.

"Get some sleep, Serena," Jacqui said and glanced at Evan. "We'll stay here and have another drink."

Chapter Twelve

The next morning Serena had breakfast with Jack, then headed to The Pearl's gardens to think. She wanted to feel close to Samurai and hoped he might possess some knowledge of the case by now. *Like a fish can help me.* Serena chuckled as she sat on the bench across from the pond. *But if any fish can, it's you, Sam.*

"Make any progress, Ms. Tate?"

Startled, Serena felt the blood rush through her veins. She would recognize that voice anywhere. It had a gruffness to it, no matter if he sounded kind or angry. "Detective." She looked up and met his steel-gray eyes. "Are you looking for me?"

"Yes." Bill Mitchell joined her on the bench.

He sat so close Serena felt the warmth of his body. She scooted away until she reached the arm rest.

"I don't bite," the detective said.

"I'm fine right here." Serena gazed towards the pond and noticed a red fish circling underwater.

"It's been almost forty-eight hours, Serena," Bill said in a natural tone. It held no animosity or disdain, as it usually did. "But, if you hear me out, I'll grand you more time." He tapped his chin. "Let's say twenty-four hours?"

"That's quite kind of you, Detective," Serena said. "Go ahead. I'll listen to what you have to say."

"I wanted to see if you've gotten any leads on your case."

"You know as much as I do, Detective Mitchell. Perhaps more."

"Please, Serena, it's Bill. We've been on enough cases that we can stop using formalities."

"Can we?" Serena closed one eye and studied the man. *What is his angle? Catch me off guard? Act friendly and hope I break? I can't text without him seeing me, but someone must notice us on the security camera. If Jack is not watching, they'll contact him.*

"You're quiet," Bill said. "I've never seen you this way. Would you like to discuss the case? Work on it together?"

Serena fidgeted in her seat. She looked around the gardens, trying to decide. *Maybe we should compare notes.*

A flash of a translucent white tail shimmered in the pond, then vanished when Serena blinked. *Sam said no. What is he? A mind reader?*

"With all the officers on the case, I'm sure you have plenty of help," Serena answered.

"The dust on the flowers was peanut butter powder," Bill replied.

That's what he chooses to share? Like we didn't know. "Common knowledge," Serena stated.

"Okay. How about this?" Bill tapped his shirt pocket. "I have the fingerprint results of the bouquet and its box right here. Would you like to see it?"

According to Sue Downing, Bill demanded exclusive access to the results. Now he wanted to share them with Serena. It made no sense, yet she said, "Sure."

"I'd be happy to show you." Bill pulled the paper from his pocket with a dramatic flair. He shook the document open and read, "The lab found five sets of fingerprints on the box. The list includes your daughter, who is currently not a suspect. Also, the deceased and the florist." He faced Serena and said, "So far, the names make sense." He cocked his head. "The other two are interesting. Evan Peterson and you, Serena."

Serena held back a gasp. She sifted through her memories, trying to recall if she touched the box. *The morning of the wedding. I moved it out of the way so nothing would happen to it.*

"My visit to The Pearl today *had* purpose. I'm taking you down to the station, Ms. Tate, for questioning."

"If you take her, then you must take Evan Peterson, too," Jack said as he walked toward them.

"How…did you…" Bill stammered. "Never mind. Fine. Have your security people escort him to the lobby, Ando. I know he's staying at the hotel."

"What happened, Bill? You gave Serena forty-eight hours to clear her name," Jack said. "Let her work on the case."

"But I've got new evidence, Jack. New evidence trumps forty-eight hours."

"No, it does not." Nina's voice rang loud and clear throughout the gardens. "You will give Serena the time she needs to complete the case, even if it takes ninety-six hours." She stared daggers at the man. "You are becoming a bully, Detective. You agreed to give Serena forty-eight hours to clear her name. However, here you are, intimidating her before the designated time. If you recall, my lawyer finalized those terms on Saturday afternoon, not Friday. Perhaps I need to make a phone call to the precinct and speak with your boss."

"Another night in lockup may have cracked you," Bill said under his breath to Serena. He rose from the bench. "You are correct as always, Mrs. Takeda. My mistake. But let me warn you, I will return when the time is up." He paused. "And to prove I am not the ogre you think I am, I have given Serena another day to work on her case." He gave a slight bow and headed for the red Torii gate.

"Nina!" Serena got up and rushed to her side. "Thank you." She took the woman's hand. "My heart is pounding, and I'm on my last nerve."

"My dear child," Nina said. "Everyone feels the stress of this case. Please tell me you've gotten a lead and are closer to discovering the killer."

"Not really." Serena hung her head. "Are you free for a visit to my office?" she asked. "You may see something we've missed." She looked at Jack. "Coming?"

"Definitely."

After the trio assembled in Serena's office, she called the tearoom and ordered tea and scones. "We can think better with a cup of tea in our hands," she said to Nina. "Please, sit."

A Pearl employee arrived within minutes, pushing a cart bearing teapots and covered dishes. "Where would you like it?" she asked.

"Against the wall." Serena pointed to an open spot by the chair. "Thank you."

Nina settled in on the sofa, and Serena served the tea. She chose to stand in front of her murder board. "Let's start with Justice's mother." She tapped Gloria's picture. "Nina, since you and Mia went to see her, what do you think? Does she stay on the board?"

"Sadly, yes." Nina held her cup in one hand as she explained. "Gloria did not want Justice to marry Tasha. She knew about the contract and the peanut allergy. Eliminating those familiar with both will provide a challenge."

"Okay." Serena turned to Jack. "I'd like to take Evan and Jacqui off the board. Do you agree?"

"Yes." Jack looked at Nina. "I'm surprised the police didn't keep Jacqui at the station or put her in a cell on Friday. She was the obvious choice as the murderer. Since they didn't lock her up, they had good reason."

"Jacqui had the means, motive and opportunity more than anyone else," Nina said. "I wondered the same thing. Why did the police let her go?"

"I'll tell you why," Jacqui leaned against the doorframe as if she'd been listening.

I can't believe I forgot to close the door. Serena gave the woman a faux smile and said, "Come in, Jacqui. We'd love to hear your answer."

"I came to speak with you, Serena, after your fishing expedition last night." Jacqui folded her arms and cocked her head. "Evan and I stayed at the bar to discuss our double date." She made air quotes with her fingers. "I said I'd help you, Serena. Why didn't you just ask? I am not guilty, but it appears you think I am."

"It's nothing against you, Jacqui. I'm trying to rule out suspects. That's all." Serena glanced at Nina, then turned to Jacqui. "Is there something you're not telling us?"

Jacqui stared at Serena as if deciding to reveal some news. "I just witnessed security take Evan from his room this morning. And yes, I stayed the night. They brought him down to the lobby, and I followed them. That grouchy detective was waiting for Evan and accused him of murdering Tasha because his fingerprints were on the box. I've had about enough of that man." She exhaled.

"Did they take him in?" Serena asked.

"No, the detective let him go after I provided some new information." Jacqui slowly let out her breath. "Let's rewind and start with the wedding day. The police took me to the station, and I answered their questions to the best of my ability. I decided not to mention Evan or that he had visited the shop. He had done nothing wrong, so why involve him? But, here's the truth. Evan stopped by early

Friday morning to help me load the van and deliver the flowers to the venue. He teased me about keeping a messy shop and used his hand to wipe the counter. Dust went flying everywhere. I realize now it wasn't dust or pollen from the flowers, as I had originally thought."

"Peanut butter powder," Serena whispered.

"Correct. If I had used the powder, would I have left traces on my counter?" Jacqui asked. "Shouldn't I have panicked when Evan ran his hand through it?"

"You would have cleaned it up and left no evidence behind," Jack answered. "That explains why the police released you on Friday."

"Yes." Jacqui nodded. "During the questioning, someone handed Detective Mitchell a folder. I assumed it was the test results. He studied the paperwork, which felt like forever." She rolled her eyes. "Probably to make me nervous. 'Peanut butter powder,' he finally said. 'They also found some on your floor and counter.' I locked eyes with him and said, 'If I had done this, would I leave evidence all over my shop?'" Jacqui blew through her lips. "He let me go home and asked if I'd return on Saturday morning to answer more questions."

"Did Mitchell let Evan go after you shared this information?" Jack asked.

"Grudgingly," Jacqui answered. "He questioned why I didn't tell him about Evan." She looked at Serena and arched her brow. "I said, 'You never asked.'"

Serena could picture Bill's face when Jacqui stood up to him. "I believe you," she said, holding back the laughter bubbling inside her. "Again, I'm sorry. I'm desperate to clear my name."

"Fine. I understand and forgive you. If you don't mind, I want to see if my boyfriend is alright. He was pretty shaken when he thought he was being arrested for killing Tasha." Jacqui glanced at the wall behind Serena. "Nice murder board." She strutted out of the office, flipping her dark blonde hair over one shoulder.

Serena gazed at Nina. "Well?"

"I believe her, too."

"Then it's two down, and how many more to go?" Serena walked to the board and removed Evan and Jacqui's photos. "Gloria, Zuri, Mandi and Shari. Who should we focus on next?"

"Shari Harrington," Nina replied.

"She won't answer my calls," Serena said.

"But she'll answer mine." Nina held up her cell phone.

* * * *

Nina was correct. Shari Harrington readily accepted a dinner invitation from the billionaire owner of The Pearl Hotel. Nina ordered the dining room chef to prepare a special meal to be served at the Takeda table. She told Jack to fit her with a wire so they could hear the conversation and reserved a special table for them.

"Shari won't notice you are there," Nina said after Jack put the wire in place. "If you lose the signal, Serena should go to the ladies' room. I will see her."

"If you can get any information, Nina, it would be wonderful," Serena said.

"I would do anything for you." Nina touched Serena's cheek. "Don't you know that by now?"

Tears welled in Serena's eyes. "And, I'd do the same. I love you, Nina."

"I love you, my dear child. I once told you that the time may come when you would need to rescue me. Well, it came, and you did. Now, it is my turn."

"We're not keeping score, Nina." Serena exhaled and folded her arms over her chest. "You don't owe me. You've done so much to help my career I can never repay you. Plus, you gave me this office and a suite upstairs."

"I thought you said we were not keeping score." Nina chuckled.

"Fine." Serena dropped her arms. "Will a hug do?"

"It sounds perfect."

"It's time," Jack said. "Places, everyone?"

* * * *

"Jack." Serena peeked over the top of her menu. "Shari has entered the building."

"What looks good for dinner tonight, Serena?"

"Did you hear me?" Serena hissed. "The eagle has landed."

"I heard you, and if you don't start acting natural, people will stare," Jack answered. He tapped his ear. "She just sat down. Nina is greeting her."

"I can hear just fine," Serena said, touching her listening device. "Nina needs to learn whether Shari was aware of the contract. It's an important piece to the puzzle. I hope Nina confronts her. Tell her she knows about the document."

"Shari could lie," Jack stated.

"True." Serena dropped her shoulders. "How will Nina discover the truth?"

"Let's listen and see."

Serena and Jack had almost finished dinner when Nina asked, "Have the police found any additional evidence in Tasha's case?" she asked.

"Finally!" Serena hissed. She widened her eyes at Jack. He shook his head but didn't speak.

"I'm glad you asked, Nina," Shari answered. "No one dares ask me about Tasha's murder, and I want to speak about it. Theo must have warned people to avoid the subject. He's afraid I will break down if I hear Tasha's name. In fact, it's just the opposite. If we don't receive some new information soon, he may be the one who has a breakdown."

"It is a difficult time," Nina replied.

"I gave the police a list of people familiar with Tasha's allergy," Shari said. "I'm trying to help in any way I can."

"Is there anything else? Something you know that might help the investigation?" Nina asked.

Serena nodded and smiled. She gave Jack the thumbs up sign.

"I wish there was," Shari continued. "I lie awake at night, searching for anything I missed."

"Did you know Theo offered Justice a job?" Nina's voice had stayed the same throughout the conversation. She kept it in control, sounding kind when needed and concerned at other times.

"Yes. Theo wanted to keep Tasha close to home, so he made this grandiose gesture to Justice, which I believe was excessive. Theo offered Justice the position of CEO of his real estate firm. I advised a gradual promotion for the man, yet Theo wouldn't budge. He believed giving Justice the job would achieve his goal."

"Did they sign a contract?" Nina asked.

"I know nothing about contracts. I'm sure it was part of the plan once Justice started work. I don't believe he had accepted the job before the wedding. Theo told me Justice was thinking it over."

Chapter Thirteen

Serena pulled the device from her ear. "Theo kept his wife in the dark. She had no clue about the arrangement."

"Perhaps Theo didn't want her involved in his shady dealings," Jack answered. He removed his earpiece and slipped it into his shirt pocket. "Shari's husband likely keeps secrets from her and shares only when it's a 'need to know' basis."

"Nina did an excellent job of leading Shari where we wanted her to go. She appears to be the concerned mother who wants her daughter's killer caught. Shari even stayed up late, making lists to help the police. I would too," Serena said.

"I don't think she's hiding anything," Jack replied. "You're right. She sounded like a grieving mother who wants answers."

"I'm right?" Serena closed one eye and tilted her head.

"Sometimes." Jack grimaced.

"Just teasing, Jack. We both have our moments. Now that we have our answers, why don't we order a bottle of wine?"

* * * *

"Please pour me one, too," Nina said, as a server added a chair to the table.

"Nina, you did a great job." Serena smiled at her.

A wine glass appeared, and Jack filled it for Nina. "I agree with Serena," he said. "Although, by the look on your face, you don't seem pleased."

"No." Nina shook her head. "It's not that. I believe the conversation went well. You only heard the conversation. I studied her expressions. It's heartbreaking. The woman is clueless, but we got the answers we needed. It's just…"

"Just what?" Serena wrinkled her nose.

"Something came to me during my conversation with Shari," Nina answered. "There is one person we've overlooked, and we should shift our focus to them." She took a sip of wine and placed the glass on the table. "Theo Harrington."

"What? Why?" Serena placed her hand over her heart. "Nina, you always surprise me."

"Think. Theo had a motive to stop the wedding. He didn't want to kill his daughter, I'm sure of that, but he needed to prevent Tasha from marrying Justice."

"Theo needed time," Jack answered, holding up his pointer finger. "He suddenly regretted the deal he had made with Justice. The contract needed to be nullified by a lawyer. He couldn't tear it up. Justice said he has a copy."

"Nina, you may need to become my sidekick," Serena teased. "I've mainly focused on the wedding party and Justice. I never thought of Theo."

"I will stick to my day job, thank you," Nina answered. She placed her hand on the table. "It is getting late. Time for me to retire. Enjoy your evening."

A server appeared and helped Nina from her chair. She wound her way through the tables and walked out of the dining room before Serena could speak. "She sure knows how to make an exit." Serena shook her head.

"And an entrance." Jack chuckled.

"How did that server sense she was about to leave?" Serena wrinkled her brow. "Don't answer. It was a rhetorical question."

"So, what's next?" Jack asked.

"I think I'll go home tonight," Serena answered. "I need to see Mama and the girls."

"Sounds like a great idea. You need a break."

"I'm not taking a break, Jack. I want to ask them questions and get a different perspective on the case. We'll sit up all night if we must."

"Then I won't keep you." Jack rose from his seat and walked to Serena's side of the table. "My lady?" He offered his hand.

Serena slipped her hand into Jack's and gazed up at him. "What would I do without you? I expected an argument, or at least..." She deepened her voice. "'Get some sleep.'"

"Do I sound like that?" Jack pouted.

"Sometimes." Serena got up and kissed his cheek. "Thanks for being understanding. I'll sleep after I solve this case."

* * * *

"I'm home," Serena called from the kitchen.

"Mom, I'm so glad you're here," Jewel said, rushing toward her. "Jade has locked herself in her bedroom and will not come out. She won't talk to us or answer our questions."

Serena engulfed her daughter in a hug, and over the top of Jewel's head, she spotted her mom.

"Jewel's right, Serena," Robin said. "Jade blames herself for everything. We can't reason with her."

"I'll speak to her," Serena answered, releasing Jewel from the hug. "We need to talk. All of us."

"Then I have a feeling we need a pot of coffee, some banana bread and lots of tissue," Robin replied. "I need to prepare for a lot of crying."

"Hopefully not." Serena grasped her mom's hand. "Do the girls drink coffee now?"

"Oh, yes. Lots of it."

"Really? Have I missed out on that much?"

"No." Robin squeezed Serena's hand. "I'm in charge of the kitchen, remember?"

Serena headed for the stairs through the front of the house. The absence of lights suggested no one was home. She strolled through the dining room and looked out the front window. "A full moon. Does that mean something?" She wrapped her arms around her body and shivered. "All will be revealed when the moon is full," she said under her breath. *Hmm, I may need to write that down.*

Serena headed to the staircase. When she arrived at the correct door, she knocked and said, "Jade?"

"Mom! I haven't seen you since Friday night." Jade threw open her door. "Are you okay?" She pulled Serena into her room and locked the door behind her.

"Yes, I am." Serena gazed at Jade. "Why lock the door?"

"I need to be alone to organize my thoughts. This is all my fault, Mom," Jade cried.

"What? No, it isn't." Serena sat on the edge of the bed. "Come here." She extended her arm so she could wrap it around Jade.

"Think, Mom. I did nothing to help. If I'd been more alert during all the wedding preparations, I may have stopped the killer or sensed who it was."

"That's why I'm here," Serena said. "Come here."

Jade snuggled against Serena, then looked at her, wrinkling her brow. "I don't understand. Why are you here instead of working on the case?"

"Will you stay up all night to discuss the case with me?"

"Of course. I'd do anything to help."

"It's the reason I came home. Not to sleep, but to work."

Jade hung her head. "I'm not a suspect anymore, but you are. Not fair."

"I have only a few more hours to prove my innocence. Jack, Nina, Mia and Lily are working hard to discover anything that might exonerate me."

"It makes no sense, Mom. I never went to the floral shop, and neither did you. We didn't know Tasha had a peanut allergy. They released me, but why not you?"

"The police found my fingerprints on the box," Serena answered. "Before this recent report, Bill Mitchell still had me at the top of his list."

"I hate him," Jade exclaimed.

"Jade, what did I tell you? We hate no one. You may dislike him but not hate him. It's such a strong word."

"Okay, then I really, really, really dislike him."

"That's my girl." Serena pulled Jade closer. "Are you ready to go downstairs?"

"Now that you're here, I can," Jade said. "I couldn't look Grandma in the eye, knowing I wasn't a suspect, and you were fighting to prove your innocence."

"Mama would never blame you, Jade." Serena kissed Jade's cheek. "I love you. You are a strong woman. Never lock yourself in a room again. We have a village to help us. Always use it."

Jade's eyes filled with tears. "You're right. I never thought of it that way."

"Do you smell coffee?" Serena asked.

"Yes." Jade giggled. "Grandma wouldn't let us stay up without something to eat."

* * * *

"I'll give you a suspect's name and time to think about them. Use these questions to help yourself. When did you see them? Did you interact with them? Did you notice anything strange about their actions?" Serena said. "Tell us everything you know. Any little detail may help."

The women had gathered in the family room, choosing comfy chairs and the sofa instead of the kitchen stools or banquette.

"Start with who you eliminated," Robin said. "We can also take them off our lists."

"Okay. There's Justice's friend, Evan. We've ruled him out." Serena held out her hand to count on her fingers. "Second is the florist. Jacqui Greene."

"I would have sworn she did it," Jewel said. "She dated Dad, had sole access to the flowers and has known Tasha since high school."

"Jacqui didn't know Tasha had a peanut allergy," Serena responded.

"Could be a lie," Jewel answered. "She must have overheard something during those years."

"If Jacqui knew, would she leave peanut butter powder all over her counter and floor?" Serena asked.

"Only if she wanted to get caught." Jewel sat forward and folded her hands. "That cleared her, didn't it?"

"Yes, and Evan."

"Who else is off your list?" Robin asked.

"Shari Harrington. Nina believes she is innocent."

"How would Nina know this?" Robin gazed at Serena.

Serena could tell her mother needed more proof. "Nina had dinner with Shari tonight. Jack and I listened in on the conversation."

"With listening devices?" Jewel rubbed her hands together.

"Yes, Jewel, with listening devices. Nina agreed to wear a mic."

"Nina is such a bad…"

"Jewel Tate! Do *not* finish that sentence," Robin cried.

"Well, she is, Gram." Jewel plopped back against the sofa cushion. "Go on, Mom. Who else?"

"That's it. Mandi and Zuri are still on my list."

"So, you're down to two suspects?" Jade asked, joining the conversation.

After not saying a word, Serena was relieved to hear Jade speak, yet she wished to withhold the identity of the third person. "Um…"

"You're leaving someone out. I can tell by your expression," Jade said. "Tell us who it is."

"Your grandmother Gloria," Serena whispered.

"What?" the girls asked in unison.

Serena swore they were about to pounce on her. The shocked looked on their faces said it all. They didn't believe Serena could accuse their grandmother of murder. *They need all the information if they are to believe me. How do I tell them about the contract?* "Mama?" She turned to Robin. "Is the coffee ready?"

"It's been ready."

"Let's go to the kitchen. While we eat, I'll tell you about Theo Harrington and Justice's agreement."

No one spoke until Serena finished the entire story. Jade gazed at her for quite a while before saying, "Dad was marrying Tasha for money. He didn't love her. I *knew* it."

"It sounds cold when you say it, Jade," Serena answered. "There's more to their story. Tasha and your dad had history."

"History of her stalking him," Jewel replied. "I bet she contacted him on the day the divorce was finalized. She seized the moment."

"I doubt it," Serena said.

"I'm siding with Jewel," Robin replied. "Tasha's father is a prominent lawyer, Serena. He could get that kind of information."

"Dad never dated Tasha until this January," Jade said, as she poured a second cup of coffee. "A few weeks later, they announced their engagement." She wrinkled her nose. "If she was available for seven or eight years…" She looked at Serena. "How long have you been divorced?"

"Since you were twelve. Seven years going on eight."

"If Tasha was so perfect for Dad, why didn't he date her right after the divorce?" Jade asked. "Don't answer. I already know. He didn't want to."

"Dad dated Jacqui for over a year," Jewel said. "I felt sorry for her. She was serious about Dad. He was not."

"Then Dad moved on to the cheerleader." Jade pointed at her sister. "Mandi."

"Hey! Why didn't you ever share this information with me?" Serena asked.

"Why? It wouldn't have changed or helped our lives," Jewel said. "Besides, we didn't know that much. We may not have seen Dad all the time, but we texted."

"You didn't get phones until you were..." Serena started putting it altogether. "Thirteen. You said it could be your only birthday present. Although I had limited funds and it was all I could afford, I wondered why you two were so content with one gift."

"Busted." Jade held up her hands, palm side up.

"Go on, Jade," Robin said. "You said Justice dated Mandi after Jacqui. What happened?"

"At first, Mandi was into Dad big time. After a month, it sounded like things cooled, and she broke things off."

Serena squinted, trying to think. "Mandi had just gotten a divorce when she started dating Justice. Maybe it was too soon. I think she said she discovered he was also seeing Tasha."

"So, let's eliminate Mandi," Jade said. "She wanted nothing to do with Dad."

"Not so fast, Ms. Tate," Serena replied. "Removing Mandi from my list requires more proof. I caught her and Zuri fighting about Justice during the rehearsal. And remember Mandi's speech? She couldn't shut up about what a great guy he is and Tasha's good fortune."

"She was drunk, Mom," Jewel said.

The girls have different perspectives, and I'm challenging everything they say. This is the exact reason I came home. I want to hear what others think. "Okay. Anything else?" Serena asked.

"Have you ever heard a drunk person reminisce about their past? They sing the blues or romanticize the past." Jewel paused. "In my opinion, that's what Mandi was doing."

"I agree," Jade said. "I swear Mandi was talking about a new man during our dress fittings. It sounded like she was really in love."

"Mandi never mentioned it to me," Serena replied and made a mental note. *Ask Mandi about a new man in her life.*

"People don't tell you everything, Mom," Jade said. "Just like you never knew we texted Dad in our younger years."

"What?" Serena placed her hand on her heart.

"We kept it from you because we thought it would upset you," Jewel said gently. "We figured you wouldn't want to hear anything about Dad. When we started spending more time with him, we'd tease him about his dating life. We learned a lot that way."

A wave of jealousy went through Serena. *Why didn't I realize this before? Since Justice reentered their lives two years ago, it's only natural the girls and Justice would form a bond. They shared stories about their daily lives when they were together.* "You girls did nothing wrong. In fact, you made the right decision. The less I knew, the better."

"We're glad you understand, Mom," Jewel said, as she stretched and yawned. "Sorry. I didn't sleep much this weekend." She stared at her sister. "I wonder why."

"I didn't mean to upset you and Gram," Jade replied. "I'm sorry, too."

"All is forgiven, girls," Robin said, clearing the counter of coffee mugs and plates. "Why don't you go to bed? Your mom and I will be up shortly."

Jade and Jewel kissed and hugged them goodnight before exiting the kitchen. After hearing their footsteps on the stairs, Robin pointed at Serena. "We've got to talk."

Chapter Fourteen

Serena's heart pounded. What could her mother say? Robin's expression gave nothing away as she rinsed the cups and placed them in the dishwasher.

"Mama, stop cleaning and tell me what's on your mind."

Robin turned to face Serena. "I'm glad we got off-topic. I didn't want to discuss Gloria in front of the girls."

"They seemed relieved to change the subject," Serena replied. "What do you want to tell me?"

"Gloria and I go to the same hair salon," Robin said. "I saw her there the week of the wedding. She was paying her bill as I walked up to the register. I could tell she was upset, so once we paid, I led her into the waiting room to talk. I must have caught her at the right time. She told me more than I should probably know. I guess Gloria needed to vent to someone."

"Mama." Serena leaned on the island, folding her hands. "What did she say?"

"Justice had shared the contract information the night before. Gloria was livid. 'No one bribes my son into marrying someone he doesn't want to,' she said with an air of defiance." Robin met Serena's eyes. "I should keep this next part to myself."

"No, Mama. Go on."

"Gloria said, 'I'd do anything to stop this marriage from happening. My son's happiness is more important than money.'"

"No!" Serena covered her mouth with her hand. "Did you tell this story to anyone else?"

Robin shook her head. "The police didn't question me for too long. Mostly I responded with 'yes' or 'no' and also provided my location at the time of Tasha's death. The detective focused mostly on you, Serena." She pointed a finger at her daughter. "Don't look at me like that. I know what you're thinking."

"If you told Detective Mitchell about Gloria, it would have helped me," Serena said. "But you weren't about to accuse someone else or turn them into the police."

"Exactly."

"I don't blame you, Mama."

Tears rolled down Robin's cheeks. "I'm sorry."

"No. Don't say that." Serena rounded the island and embraced her mom. "I would have done the same thing. I'll solve this case, Mama. Don't you worry."

"You only have a few more hours, Serena." Robin stepped back and gave Serena a stern look. "You clear your name, my sweet girl, and I'll be the first one to dance into that detective's office with the biggest grin on my face to say, 'I told you so.'"

* * * *

Despite a restless night, Serena was grateful to lie in the quiet darkness. If she could just clear her mind, she might sleep, yet it never happened. Finally, she got up before the alarm she'd set and popped into the shower. Dressed and ready for the day, Serena called Jack to update him.

"I plan to drive to Gloria's house and surprise her. It won't give her time to make up excuses," Serena said.

"Excellent plan," Jack replied. "Are you coming to the hotel after the visit?"

"Yes, please inform the others I'll be ready to meet and discuss the next step in our plan. I hope this goes well."

"Call if you need me, Serena. I wish you luck."

Serena ended the call and opened her bedroom door to discover her mom in the hallway. "Mama," she whispered. "I'm sneaking out."

"I figured you would," Robin said. "Go. Do your job." She stepped back and let Serena pass.

"Love you." Serena touched her mom's arm as she went by her.

"Love you more," Robin responded. "Go easy on her, Serena."

Serena tiptoed through the hall to avoid waking the girls as she went from house to garage. She slipped behind the driver's seat and started the engine. Taking a deep breath, she backed the car into the street and headed for the Tate home fifteen minutes away.

Before reaching the house, Serena spotted a familiar car in the driveway. *Justice.* She stopped and parked behind an SUV further down the street. Justice came out, opened the driver's side and leaned down, appearing to speak with someone inside the car. Then Justice hopped in and sped away. When he drove by, Serena slumped down below window level so he wouldn't see her.

Once he passed her, Serena sat up and checked the rearview mirror. "Someone else is in the car with him. But who exactly?" She made a face in the mirror. "Could be nothing."

Pulling into the Tate's driveway, Serena checked the time. "Almost nine a.m. I hope Gloria's awake." She gripped the steering wheel and stared at the house. "You can do this, Serena."

Serena marched to the front door and rang the bell. Within seconds, the door swung open.

"Justice, did you forget some…?" Gloria tightened her bathrobe around her neck. "Serena. What are you doing here?"

"May I come in, Gloria?" Serena asked.

"Where are my manners?" Gloria stepped aside. "Of course. Please come in."

The home's familiarity overwhelmed Serena. The Tates hadn't changed a thing or updated the room since the last time she visited before her divorce. Each piece of furniture remained in the same place, and the walls were the same color. Serena shook her head to focus.

"Can I get you anything?" Gloria asked.

"No, thanks," Serena answered. "I'm only staying a few minutes."

"You spoke with your mother," Gloria said in a knowing tone.

Serena tried to give Gloria an innocent look.

"Serena Tate." Gloria folded her arms. "I've known you since high school. Your expression suggests you're up to something."

Serena pursed her lips and sighed. "Yes, I want to ask you a few questions."

"Ask away. I have nothing to hide."

"You told my mom you'd do anything to protect Justice," Serena replied. "Looks like you didn't approve of the marriage."

Gloria let out a sharp breath. "I'll admit I wasn't thrilled about the situation, but I would never kill the woman."

"Of course not," Serena agreed. "But stop the wedding?" She lifted her brows. "Perhaps."

"I already spoke to your friends, Serena. They believed me, right?"

"They were collecting facts, Gloria, not deciding guilt or innocence," Serena answered. "Honestly? Anyone aware of Tasha's allergy and the contract is a suspect."

"Did you hear this from the police?" Gloria asked in a concerned voice.

"No. I'm conducting my own research." Serena closed her eyes and slowly opened them. "I don't think you did it, Gloria. I'm here for two reasons." She held up the correct number of fingers. "Tell no one about your conversation with Mama. She will never reveal the contents of that conversation either."

"And the second?"

"It's crucial you speak with Justice. If the authorities uncover the deal between him and Theo, he cannot reveal who else knows about the contract. They will instantly become a suspect."

"Oh." Gloria touched her chin. "He won't, but I'll speak to him."

Perfect opportunity to ask about him. "On my way here, I thought I saw him driving away from your house."

"Yes, Justice is staying with us for a few weeks," Gloria answered. "Too many nosy people lurking outside his condo."

"The media?" Serena asked.

"I guess." Gloria lifted her shoulder.

"I suppose you don't have any peanut butter powder in the house?" Serena teased.

"Serena!" The sides of Gloria's mouth twitched.

"I had to ask." Serena wrinkled her nose. "From one mama bear to another, I understand you want to protect your child. But if you think of anything that could help me, please call or text." She embraced Gloria, inhaling the familiar scent of roses. "Still using the same shower gel?"

"My favorite." Gloria hugged her tighter. "Just as you are."

* * * *

"I had to see Gloria for myself. Speak with her face to face," Serena informed the group gathered in her office. Her eyes landed on a breakfast buffet in front of her desk. "But first…" She gestured toward the buffet.

The staff had set up a table so the main restaurant could serve a continental breakfast. Serena chose a croissant to pair with her coffee. "Thanks, Jack," she murmured as she passed by him.

"I figured you hadn't eaten," Jack said with a playful wink.

"Let's start with your visit to Gloria," Nina announced after Serena took her seat. "Jack informed us about your mother's conversation with Robin, which we will keep confidential."

"I knew you would," Serena replied. "I don't believe Gloria is responsible for Tasha's death, but I needed to talk to her, warn her. The less said, the better."

"Are you taking Gloria off your list?" Mia asked.

"Yes." Serena approached her board. "Which leaves Mandi and Zuri."

"Don't forget Theo Harrington," Lily added. "Nina thinks he may know who did it or hired someone to apply the powder."

"I agree," Serena said, "But I don't know where to start with him. I can't call him. He will report me to Bill Mitchell. The detective seems to go out of his way to pacify the man and do as he asks."

"Okay," Mia said. "Our next task is figuring out a way to speak with Theo Harrington without police involvement. Meanwhile, what is your plan, Serena? You can't waste a minute."

"I'm aware the clock is ticking," Serena said with a sigh. "I must get Zuri and Mandi together and see if one of them breaks or reveals new information."

"Before anyone leaves," Jack said. "I want to hear your opinions on my theory. What if there are multiple people involved? Two people could work together. For example, Jacqui and Evan. Do you see what I mean?"

"Even Zuri and Mandi could have conspired," Serena replied. "It makes sense, Jack. I'll use a few different tactics when I speak with them. I was going to use, divide and conquer but will add another. Friendship."

* * * *

When Serena stepped into the lobby, she found it bustling with people. Bellmen pushed carts full of luggage toward the exit, while some guests wheeled their own out the door. "Check out time," she said under her breath.

Serena hoped to have a peaceful moment in the garden and mumbled under her breath, "If I could only reach the Torii gate." She decided not to let the crowds deter her and pressed on. *The gardens are where I do my best thinking.*

She wanted to sit on the bench near the pond to review her new findings. Sam would be nearby to help, if needed. From there, she'd send a text to Zuri and Mandi, hoping they'd agree to see her.

As she dodged rolling luggage and groups of people leaving the building, Serena tried to walk a straight path to the red Torii gate. She paused, yielding to individuals oblivious to her or anything going on in the hotel. After a near collision, Serena almost gave up. *Am I invisible?*

Serena felt a strong hand grasp her arm just above the elbow. "Excuse me, Ms. Tate," a man's voice said. "Please come with me."

After a useless struggle to free her arm, Serena faced the man. "Let go," she growled.

The man, dressed in street clothes, flashed a police badge. "This way." He tugged on her arm.

When they stepped outside, a cool breeze greeted them, wafting in from the Pacific Ocean. It carried the faint smell of salt and sea air. The iconic fog, known to the locals as "Karl", had almost lifted, and the sun cast golden light through the mist.

Serena's heightened senses heard the clang of the trolley and the hum of morning traffic as they walked along the outside of the hotel. She inhaled the aroma of freshly brewed coffee and baked goods from the shops down the street. Though her heart was pounding, the familiar smells helped slow her breathing and focus on what was to come.

The officer led her to a black car and opened the back door.

"I'm not getting in there," Serena hissed. "It's not an official police cruiser."

"It's unmarked," the man answered. "Would you prefer an officer in uniform and flashing lights on a cruiser instead?"

Serena eyed the man carefully. "You think of everything. This car better drive to the station. I know the way."

"I'm sure you do," the officer answered, appearing to hold back a smile.

Once inside the police station, the man guided her to Bill Mitchell's office. He sat behind his desk, coffee mug in hand, and grinned when he saw Serena. "Welcome, Ms. Tate. I finally have you all to myself."

"That sounds like a lawsuit." Serena smirked.

Bill rose from his chair and yelled, "You *know* what I mean." He inhaled and said, "Are you aware your forty-eight hours has ended?"

"I thought it was more opened-ended, not locked down to the exact minute. I still need time to interview two suspects."

Bill Mitchell's expression said otherwise. "Take her to a cell and lock her up, Abe. Thanks for your help."

"Can't we talk now so I can be on my way?" Serena asked as the officer pulled her toward the door.

"No." Bill shook his head. "A few hours in lock up will give you time to reflect. Confess, and this ends today."

"I have nothing to confess," Serena said in a calm voice.

"Fine. Then, enjoy the quiet time. Rest up." Bill smiled, but it didn't reach his eyes. "I'll see you in about..." He checked his watch. "Two hours?"

Chapter Fifteen

Serena paced the floor, sat on the cot, got up and paced some more. "Hotel security must have seen me. But then again, a dense crowd filled the lobby. I'm sure Bill planned it that way." She put her palms together. "Please, Jack, find me or wonder why I haven't contacted you." Serena sighed and returned to the cot. "Stop feeling sorry for yourself and come up with a plan."

A door slammed, and Serena jumped from the cot. She would not sit while Bill interrogated her. They would speak face to face, despite the bars between them. Serena wrapped her hands around them and waited.

"I thought I'd find you napping," Bill said as he approached.

"Cut to the reason you want to talk," Serena replied.

"Look." Bill threw out his hands. "I know you did it. *You* know you did it. Let's end the charade now. You're the jealous ex-wife forced to become the wedding planner. We have footage of you entering a grocery store that sells peanut butter powder, and your fingerprints are on the bouquet box. I think our district attorney can present an open and shut case."

When he puts it like that, the facts seem damaging, but insufficient for a conviction. Fight, Serena, fight. Serena tilted her head. "You've been hard at work, Detective. I'm sure that profile fits many people who attended the wedding."

"True." Bill folded his arms over his protruding belly. "But none have motive like you do."

Serena glanced around the cell. "Can we speak somewhere more private? I need to tell you something no one else should hear."

Bill lifted his brows and dropped his arms to his sides. "I'm listening."

"Not here." Serena stared at him. "Yesterday, you said you wanted to work together. Today, I'm accepting your offer. Do you want to solve the case and get full credit?"

"You'll stay out of the way? Hard to believe."

"You have my word." Serena held up one hand.

"Fine. We'll talk. But if I don't like it, you're coming straight back to this cell."

* * * *

A police officer escorted Serena to a room with no two-way mirror or listening devices. *Does this mean I can trust him?* While she sat waiting for Bill Mitchell, she hoped Jack wouldn't find her too soon. She had devised a plan and intended to see it through. "Not to trick you, Bill, but to *really* work together," Serena whispered.

The door swung open, and Bill hesitated in the entryway. "No games, right? Mrs. Takeda won't come bursting in here or Jack Ando playing Superman."

His comment made Serena smile. "I can't say, Detective. Do they know I'm here?"

Bill shrugged as he took the seat across from Serena. "Start talking, and this better be good."

"This concerns Theo Harrington." Serena held up her pointer finger. "Before you defend the man, hear me out."

"The man lost his daughter." Bill shook his head. "I can't believe he murdered her."

"He didn't. Now, if you'd please let me finish?" Serena waited for Bill to speak, but he remained silent. "You're siding with Harrington because you hope he can do for you what Nina hasn't—get you a promotion. Perhaps he has offered more, but you must listen with an open mind."

"Okay." Bill placed his hands on the table. "What can you tell me about Theo Harrington that he hasn't?"

"Harrington offered Justice the position of CEO of his real estate firm if Justice agreed to marry Tasha. I believe Theo had second thoughts and wanted to stop the wedding. The two parties had already signed the contract, so he required time to have it legally nullified. Being a lawyer himself, Theo was aware of what needed to be done. He couldn't rip it up like they do in the movies."

Bill slapped the table. "Who shared this information with you without telling me?"

Serena closed one eye and pursed her lips. "Do I need to spell it out?"

"Everyone is afraid of me?"

"No." Serena shook her head. "It's quite simple. You are the police. No one would willingly divulge this kind of information to you."

"Whatever." Bill scowled. "Go on."

"My theory is that Theo hired someone to taint the bouquet. The person overdid the dosage, and you know the rest."

Bill leaned forward. "You almost make sense, Serena. How can I get my hands on this contract?"

"Theo may have shredded the document, but I bet Justice still has his. If I'm correct, you'll need to get a court order to retrieve the document. That might take time. Once you have the contract, call in a list of suspects I give you, including myself. Meanwhile, release me and let me pursue the questioning of two more suspects."

"I thought the contract was the answer," Bill said, tapping the table with his finger. "The proof I needed to solve this case."

"It *could* be the answer," Serena replied. "But I must eliminate every suspect before we focus on Theo Harrington. How soon can you get this done?"

"It won't take long. I'll have everything by tomorrow," Bill answered. "Don't make me regret this."

"Once you have the contract, contact me. I won't warn Justice about what's coming, but I will ask him to stay silent afterwards. Text me. Don't call. This is between you and me, Bill. Our staged intervention must look real. I won't even tell Jack or Nina."

Bill lifted his brows. "You're serious?"

"I want Tasha's killer caught just as much as you do, Detective, and I don't care who gets the credit. Partnering with you wasn't in my plans. It is now. Take it or leave it."

"You are free to go, Ms. Tate. I will have an officer drive you back to The Pearl Hotel."

"I appreciate that," Serena replied. "At your convenience."

* * * *

After being dropped off at The Pearl, Serena headed for the gardens. She stopped at the pond and rested her hands on the fence which surrounded it. "Sam," she hissed. "Are you there?"

The koi's red head popped from the water. Serena thought he wore a worried expression. "Are you okay?" The fish dunked his head underwater and emerged again. "Was Jack looking for me?" Again, Samurai performed the same moves. "I'm fine, Sam, and still working on the case. I messaged Zuri and Mandi, inviting them to the tearoom. I made it sound urgent. Neither knows the other is coming."

Sam swam in rapid circles around the pond, finally coming to a stop in front of Serena. "You don't like what is happening, either. I've usually solved the mystery by now. Don't worry, I'm getting close. Putting Zuri and Mandi together might help." She leaned over the railing. "They may give conflicting stories or became allies. Let's see if I can uncover the truth."

"Serena, there you are," Jack's voice came from the main path. "Before I spotted you, I was on my way to security to see if someone abducted you," he chuckled.

"Who would do that?" Serena smiled at Jack, knowing he was close to the truth.

"It's happened before." Jack placed his hands on his hips.

"Did you check my room?" Serena asked.

"No." Jack dropped his head. "Is that where you were?"

"Yes," Serena lied.

"You didn't answer my texts."

"I fell asleep." Serena glanced over her shoulder and gestured at the tearoom. "I'm meeting Zuri and Mandi there in fifteen minutes. Let's sit. I've got a little time." She approached the bench and sat, patting the seat next to her.

Jack slid in beside her. "It's not like you to nap during an investigation. Are you okay?" He felt her forehead.

"Jack." Serena removed his hand. "I'm not a kid. If I was sick, I would tell you. I didn't mean to fall asleep. It just happened. After my calls to Zuri and Mandi, I lay back on the bed. Before I knew it, two hours had gone by."

"It seems more like four." Jack squinted and looked up at the ceiling. "Anyway, I found you." He took her hand and wrinkled his brow. "I just realized your forty-eight hours has ended, and you're still here."

"I called Bill and begged for one more day," Serena answered. "I was shocked when he gave his approval. Now I must take advantage of the extra time."

"Then I don't want to keep you," Jack squeezed her hand. "Give me instructions. Tell me what you want me to do."

"Carry me back upstairs," Serena teased.

"Besides that."

"Just be you, Jack. When the time comes, be open to whatever unfolds."

"That sounds ominous."

"Does it?" Serena wrinkled her nose. "I didn't mean it to be." She squeezed his hand. "I love you."

"I love you now and forever," Jack answered. He pointed to the pond. "Despite my attempts to lure Samurai from the depths of the pond, I had no luck. I had hoped he would help me find you. That fish is loyal to you, Serena. You visited him before going upstairs, I take it?"

"Yes, I always need my Sam time." Serena saw Sam's white tail appear above the water. *Don't show yourself now, Sam. Especially since Jack would realize that's a 'no' answer.*

"Before I leave, I need my instructions, Ms. Tate," Jack used a formal voice, then chuckled.

"I should be in the tearoom for several hours. Let's meet for dinner. After that, I plan to sleep for at least ten hours."

"Aren't you concerned Bill will go back on his promise and come for you?" Jack asked.

"Oh! I forgot to tell you. During our call, our friendly detective said I can report to jail in the morning. Isn't that big of him?"

Jack gazed at Serena longer than she liked, yet she kept a smile in place. "We can be alone tonight, Jack, before I head to the Big House."

"Serena." Jack stood and pulled Serena to her feet. "It will not happen. I won't let it."

"How?"

"We tell Mitchell about the contract."

No. No. No. "If we must. But let's not go there yet." Serena kissed Jack, not caring who saw. She slid her hands across his shoulders and up into his hair. "Trust me," she whispered, hoping he wouldn't ask more questions.

Serena stepped back and locked eyes with Jack. She let go of him and headed for the main path, praying he wouldn't follow.

* * * *

Serena took her time walking along the flagstone path. She soaked in the beauty and serenity of the gardens. *What if I go to jail? I may never stroll through these gardens again.* Tears filled her eyes. *I need to commit this place to memory so I can conjure it up wherever I am. I have walked through these gardens many times, but did I truly see them?*

"Built to bring nature inside," Serena whispered.

The designers had used stone for landscape walls, and in one area, created a Zen rock garden. The flagstone pathways encouraged mindful walking, winding through the gardens to various shops and restaurants. Bonsai trees, moss and ferns added a pop of green among the cherry blossom trees and azaleas. Soft lighting, along with a skylight, gave off an inviting ambiance. *How did I not notice?*

Serena approached the tea house with reverence and respect. She had visited this place countless times and never appreciated it. She had taken it all for granted. Before entering, Serena took calming breaths and inhaled the jasmine scent.

Jun had seated Zuri at the Takeda table in the tearoom's back corner. Serena waved and acted casually as she approached. She took a seat and said, "I'm glad you came."

"You made it sound like I didn't have a choice," Zuri huffed.

"Before Mandi gets here, I must ask you something," Serena said.

"Mandi's coming?" Zuri began to rise from her chair.

"Please, Zuri, stay. I need your help."

"Fine." Zuri dropped back into her seat. "What's your question?"

"Does Mandi know about the contract?"

Zuri's eyes widened, and she wrapped her hands around her teacup. "I don't think so."

"You are still close to Justice. Surely, he told you about the document."

"He told me about the contract in confidence," Zuri stated. "If he chose to inform Mandi, that's his business."

"After all those years, were you surprised when Tasha and Mandi's friendship changed?"

"You mean after Mandi's divorce?" Zuri asked. "Yeah, but Mandi didn't seem to care."

"Did Tasha?"

"Yes, and no. She never spoke about their friendship until Mandi unexpectedly reappeared in her life."

"A year ago," Serena responded.

"They made up. What can I say?" Zuri rolled her eyes and snarled. "Here she comes."

"Please stay for one more question," Serena begged. *So much for the friends' idea.*

"Hello, Serena. You didn't tell me *she* would be here," Mandi said, her voice dripping with disdain.

"Zuri was in the tearoom, and I invited her to sit with me. I assumed you wouldn't mind," Serena said, acting as if she didn't see a problem.

"I was just going," Zuri said. "But since we're both here, Serena wanted to ask us something. I'd do anything to help her clear her name. Wouldn't you?'

"Sure." Mandi pulled out a chair and sat down. "Do I get some tea?"

"Absolutely." Serena motioned for Jun, and the woman arrived at lightning speed. "Jun, some English Breakfast for the table and some scones."

Jun widened her eyes yet said nothing. She nodded and left before Serena could thank her. *Nina's around here somewhere. I can feel her presence. Jun is probably reporting to her now.*

"Zuri." Serena gazed at the woman. "Mandi." She faced the other. "What were you fighting about rehearsal night? Please, be truthful."

"I'll start," Mandi said. "I was trying to convince Ms. Mensa here that I wasn't interested in Justice. She could have him."

"Just because I'm smart doesn't mean you should mock me. It's an honor to be part of Mensa International," Zuri commented. "So what if I'm smart? Having an IQ of over one hundred thirty doesn't help my personal life."

"Aww, let's feel sorry for you." Mandi smirked.

"Stop." Serena held up a hand. "Can we get back to the fight?" She turned to Zuri. "Mandi told you she wasn't interested in Justice, so why argue?"

"She lied." Zuri pointed a finger at Mandi. "She went on and on about some man during our dress fittings. I couldn't take it anymore and wanted Mandi to admit it was Justice."

The girls were right. "What if it wasn't Justice, and Mandi told the truth?" Serena asked.

"I'm finished with this interrogation." Zuri threw her napkin on the table. "Goodbye, Serena, and I wish you luck. You are in a terrible spot, and I don't envy you. Forty-eight hours to clear your name was not enough time." She pushed back her chair and headed for the exit.

How did she know I had forty-eight hours to clear my name? Did I tell her? Or Justice? If he did, he contacted her after my Friday release.

"Serena." Mandi placed a hand on her arm. "Are you alright? It seems like I lost you for a second."

"I'm fine." Serena sat back as Jun placed teapots and a two-tiered serving dish filled with tiny croissants and muffins on the table. "Thanks, Jun. Is Nina here?"

Jun wrinkled her brow. "I don't believe so." She touched Serena's shoulder. "If I see her, should I send her over?"

"Just inform her I'm doing well. No need to worry." Serena turned to Mandi. "Who is telling the truth? You or Zuri?"

Chapter Sixteen

"Why, Serena Tate." Mandi's jaw dropped. "How can you ask such a thing? Who is telling the truth? Me or Zuri?" She touched her chest and giggled. "Haven't I always told the truth?"

"No." Serena bit her lip. "I get your point. No one always tells the truth."

"There you have it," Mandi replied, pouring a cup of tea. "It comes down to this. Who will you believe?"

"I'm trying to wade through this mess and make some sense of it, Mandi. What's the truth about you and Justice?"

Mandi stirred a teaspoon of sugar into her tea. "When my marriage fell apart, Justice was there for me. As I said, we dated for about a month. It didn't work out. Funny, isn't it? I had the man I thought I loved and needed all those years ago. Then, poof. The dream was better than the man."

"Justice and I spoke about the days after your divorce, Mandi. He said Tasha never gave you any financial help during that time."

"What does he know? It's a girl code thing," Mandi smirked. "We kept it between us. Also, if Tasha's dad discovered what she was doing, he would have halted the cash flow. Poor little Mandi. She's in trouble again and needs Tasha's help. It proves what kind of friend she was. She bailed me out and never told a soul."

"I heard you two had a falling out and never spoke until a year ago," Serena said. "Did Tasha provide you with money during the time you didn't speak?"

"Who told you that?" Mandi appeared irritated. "We communicated mostly through texts. I was going through a rough time. The divorce took a lot out of me. I had to move in with my parents. Find a job. Lucky for me, my mom watched my daughter while I worked."

"Part time," Serena added.

"So?"

"You moved into a condo two years later. Did you use the money Tasha gave you or was it from this high-paying part-time job?"

"I never said how much I make," Mandi answered with a sigh. "I don't see how this pertains to your case. As Zuri said, I am rooting for you, Serena. Other than that, I have nothing more to add."

"Serena!' Justice appeared at the table. "Oh, hello, Mandi. I didn't expect to see you." He faced Serena. "We need to talk."

"Don't let me stop you," Mandi said. "I was just leaving."

"Wait." Serena rose from her chair. "Since you're both here, perhaps Justice can answer some questions which also concern you, Mandi."

Mandi narrowed her eyes and hissed, "Really?"

"Yes, really." Serena folded her arms across her chest. "Justice, you said Tasha never gave Mandi money after her divorce. Am I right or did I not hear you correctly?"

"You heard me correctly," Justice answered. "Something happened between you and Tasha, Mandi." He shook his finger at her. "Tasha never offered an explanation, but she ended the friendship. She never gave you a dime."

"She did, Justice. Tasha didn't want you to know because *you'd* start asking for money." Mandi got up and pushed through Justice and Serena. "I'm done here."

"Whoa, she's mad," Justice said as he met Serena's eyes. "No matter what Mandi says, I'm telling the truth."

"Funny," Serena smirked. "I rarely believe a word coming from your charming mouth, but I do now."

"I'm charming?" Justice fluttered his lashes.

Serena tapped his arm. "Stop it. Walk the gardens with me. I want to spend as much time there as I can."

"Hey, you will not go to jail," Justice replied as they stepped into the gardens. "*If* that's what you're implying."

The two walked in silence until they reached the pond. Serena chose the spot on purpose, hoping Sam would hear their conversation. She sat on her bench and stared at the fountain, gracefully spraying water into the air before the drops landed in the pond. "My favorite spot," Serena said. She looked at Justice. "What did you want to tell me?"

"I got a court order to produce the contract I signed with Theo Harrington's real estate company. I have until tomorrow to hand it over to Detective Mitchell. How on earth did he find out?" Justice rubbed the spot between his eyes.

"I told him," Serena admitted.

"Serena!" Justice glared at her. "I told you about the contract in strict confidence."

"I'm sorry, Justice. Giving Mitchell the contract will help solve the case."

"Yeah, right," Justice snarled. "All you did is shift his focus back on me. Free you and indict me. Am I right?"

"No. It won't happen. Trust me." Serena patted Justice's hand. "I've always had your best interests at heart, haven't I?"

"Yes," Justice mumbled. "Does Harrington know about this?"

"No, and please don't tell him."

"You're up to something, Serena. Spill."

Serena needed to invent a story Justice would believe. *Always tell a partial truth.* "Our favorite detective hauled me into the station this morning. He claimed to have fresh evidence and stuck me in a holding cell for two hours, hoping I would crack. All it did was waste the valuable time I needed to wrap up my investigation."

"Mitchell is sneaky, Serena. He'd do anything to solve this case before you. He put you in the cell to waste time."

"True." Serena nodded. "When Mitchell visited my cell, he said he felt Harrington was hiding something and was determined to uncover the truth. Mitchell plans to bring everyone in for more questioning and keep them at the station until he solves the mystery."

"Since my mom and Zuri knew, you're hoping one of them will break and tell Mitchell about the contract," Justice growled.

"Perhaps." Serena lifted her shoulder. "But I sensed Mitchell already knew, so I insisted on speaking with him privately. We met in a room, just the two of us, and he admitted to receiving critical information and needed verification. The more I probed, he finally revealed what he'd been hiding. The missing piece. The contract," she fibbed. "I don't want Jewel and Jade to be escorted to the station again or your mom, Justice. I only confirmed what he already knew."

Justice didn't seem convinced. He stood, looking down at Serena with fire in his eyes. "I'll go home, get the contract and take it to the station." He gazed at her until she felt uncomfortable. "You better be right, Serena. My mom's freedom is on the line," he growled before storming down the path.

"I hope I am," Serena whispered.

* * * *

"Mama?"

"Serena, baby, is that you?" Robin replied. "Are you okay? You sound like you are crying."

"No, I'm not alright, and yes, I am crying," Serena answered. "I would drive home but don't have time. Can you come to The Pearl? I need you."

"My car keys are in my hand, sweetheart. Where should I meet you?"

"My suite. I'll wait for you there."

"I hope the traffic is light. See you in a half hour."

Since things did not go well with Justice, Serena wished to avoid Jack and any prying questions. "Jack has a job. Hopefully, he's busy with Pearl business," she said under her breath as she headed for the elevator hallway.

Once inside her room, Serena leaned against the door, taking deep, measured breaths. Her mind reeled as she struggled to process what she had learned today. "How will tomorrow's meeting go?" She shook her head. "Too many unknown factors. I need to be prepared for anything."

A tapping noise startled Serena, and she moved away from the door. *How long have I been standing there?* "Mama?" she called.

"Yes, it's me."

Serena opened the door and fell into her mom's arms. She couldn't stop crying, and Robin let her weep on her shoulder until she gasped for breath.

"Let's sit down, shall we?" Robin's voice was calm and soothing. "Here's a tissue, baby girl. This must be important, so start talking."

"I'm a mess," Serena cried. "I have no idea what I am doing or the direction of this case. I came up with this grandiose plan that I hope works. Do you hear me? I said *hope.* I'm not sure of anything. Usually, I'm setting up a suspect to get them to confess, but I'm still torn over who killed Tasha. This could go terribly wrong."

"Serena Elizabeth Baker-Tate." Robin took her hand. "What's happened to my force of nature? You let no one down. Look at how you fought for your girls and Nina during their struggles. Isn't it time to do it for yourself?"

"It's not the same," Serena mumbled.

"Not the same? Yes, it is. You're scared, baby. I understand." Robin placed her hands on Serena's cheeks. "Look at me. Swear you won't give up. Fight like you did for your family and friends. You deserve equal treatment."

"I never thought of it that way." Serena sniffed. "I saw myself as some sort of superhero, rescuing family and friends."

"Put that cape on again, Serena. For *you.*" Robin exhaled. "After you're vindicated, why don't you take a break? Go back to writing those wonderful books."

Serena gave a humorless laugh. "It's not that simple, Mama. Writing is hard. I've got four books out there. I'm good with that."

"You're going to stop writing?"

"Not exactly. I need a break from it all. Amateur detective. Author. What was I thinking?"

"I won't let you stop." Robin folded her arms. "The world needs your contributions. I understand you are tired and demoralized. What you need is a good night's rest. Things will appear brighter tomorrow."

"Easy for you to say," Serena snickered.

"I can stay overnight if you like," Robin said.

"No, I'd rather have you home with the girls. I'll feel much better knowing you're there. Thanks for coming so quickly." Serena hugged her mom. "I will fight for myself, Mama. I promise."

"Pinkie swear?" Robin winked and held up her little finger.

"Pinkie swear."

* * * *

After reassuring her mom she would be alright and sent her on her way, Serena flipped on the TV for background noise and got to work. "First, text Jack." She reached for her phone and saw she had a message. "Bill Mitchell." She opened the text and read, "List ready to go? Would like it now."

Slapping the sofa cushion, Serena said, "Ooh, that man is exasperating. Why did I agree to work with him? You'll have to wait, Detective. Someone is more important than you."

Serena dashed off a message to Jack, giving him enough information so he wouldn't worry. She finished by inviting him to breakfast in the tearoom along with Mia and Lily. It was the perfect place for Bill to arrest her and make it believable.

"I hope you're an excellent actor, Bill. You have a huge part to play in this final scene." Serena tapped his message and began to type her list. "Send." She waited to see if he'd answer.

His text arrived after a short wait. "I'll have everyone brought in by ten a.m. Anything else?"

"Yes, arrest me in the tearoom before that. Make sure to invite Theo Harrington to the station as an observer. We don't want him to think he's a suspect."

"O.K."

Serena rolled her eyes and spoke to the screen. "That's it? Okay spelled like that?"

Since she couldn't sleep, Serena got a pen and paper and settled back in front of the television. The local news, weather and sports finished, and she still hadn't written a thing. She scribbled questions to ask the group. "What would make someone do this?" Serena mumbled, then recalled her mother's words. *Look at how you fought for your girls and Nina when they were in trouble.*

"And why did I do that?" Serena tapped the pen against her chin. "Love." Exhaustion crept in, but frustration kept her going. "Zuri loves Justice, and Mandi loved him but has moved on. Theo loved his daughter and would do anything for her. Wait a minute...that's it! I know who did it."

Serena dropped onto the sofa in celebration, hugging herself. "I think I can finally rest." She took her phone off the coffee table and set an alarm. Not able to pull herself off the couch, Serena let herself drift off into a dreamless sleep.

Chapter Seventeen

"I'm so glad to see you," Lily cried, hopping up from her chair. "Mia and I thought you returned to prison last night without saying goodbye. When we got your text this morning, we couldn't believe it." She embraced Serena in a bear hug. "Kudos, my friend, you outsmarted Bill Mitchell. He saw the error of his ways and let you go."

"Not exactly," Serena replied, turning to Mia, who waited for a hug. "But I need all my available free time to solve this case."

"Are you close?" Mia asked.

"I'm down to three suspects," Serena answered. "So… no."

"Oh. Sorry to hear." Mia gestured to the table. "Please, let's sit. Perhaps we can help. Jun will serve breakfast shortly."

"I hope you don't mind, but I invited Jack to join us. I didn't see him last night. Instead, I went to my room to focus on the case."

"Say no more." Mia held up her hand, and Jun appeared. "There's will be one more for breakfast, Jun, and I believe his tea preference is Sencha."

"Very well." Jun smiled and nodded.

"Before Jack gets here, tell us what happened yesterday. We didn't see you all day," Lily said.

"Since you are my P.I.C. partners, I'm going to tell you the truth because I'll need your help later," Serena replied. "Sit back and relax. It's a long story. I hope to finish before Jack arrives. I gave him a later breakfast time."

"I can see the entrance from here," Mia said. "I'll watch for him. Go ahead. We're listening."

Serena exhaled. "Monday night I went home to check on everyone. Mama had withheld some important details about Gloria, so the next morning I stopped by Justice's house. I needed to speak with his mom." Serena recounted her morning activity and her visit to the Tate house. "I returned here and met with Jack and Nina in my office. Things went according to plan until a plain clothes detective intercepted me on my way to the tearoom."

"No-o-o," Lily sneered. "Bill Mitchell doesn't play fair." She closed one eye and tilted her head. "How did security miss this?"

"It was checkout time," Serena answered. "People everywhere. I don't think anyone watching the monitors could have picked me out of the crowd unless they were looking for me." She lifted her shoulder. "Anyway, the detective took me in an unmarked car to the station."

"Wow. Sounds well-planned," Lily said.

"I agree," replied Serena. "The detective took me to Mitchell's office. Instead of having a quick chat, he put me in a holding cell for two hours."

"He is such a…" Mia pounded a fist on the table.

"It's alright, Mia." Serena covered Mia's dainty fist with her hand. "It gave me time to think. I decided on a fresh approach. Work with the man."

"Whoa." Lily lifted her brows. "Did he agree?"

"After much persuasion and presenting new evidence, he finally agreed."

"The contract?" Lily stared at her. "You didn't."

"I did." Serena nodded.

Jun arrived with tea and scones for the women. She poured tea and placed the freshly baked scones on the table. "You may speak in front of me. I am also interested in the case." She winked and left as the women's jaws dropped open.

"I knew it. She is Nina's spy," Serena said. "Think about it. Nina's timing is uncanny. How does she know when to appear at our table? I bet Jun calls and tells her we are here."

"I wouldn't go that far," Mia chuckled. "But somehow Grandmother finds out everything."

"I still say Nina was a ninja in another life," Serena responded. "Or a magician. Poof! She appears."

The women laughed and put their conversation on hold to enjoy the scones. Serena poured another cup of tea, enjoying the scent before taking a sip. "If I end up in jail, please sneak in some oolong for me," she said, half-kidding.

"Serena!" Mia shook her head. "That won't happen. Let's return to the case. What do you want us to do?"

"When Mitchell arrives, you must look outraged and act accordingly. Neither Jack nor Nina can follow me to the police station. If they try, you must stop them. I can't have allies in the interrogation room or someone trying to negotiate my freedom. I need to look guilty."

"We understand." Mia widened her eyes. "Jack is here." She smiled brightly as he placed his hands on Serena's shoulders. "Hi, Jack," she said. "Please join us."

"I only have an hour," Jack answered, taking the open seat. "Scones look good."

"Help yourself," Mia said. "Jun is bringing your tea."

The group ordered breakfast crepes and another round of tea. Afraid Jack would be suspicious if she didn't discuss the case, Serena shared Jade and Jewel's thoughts after speaking with them on Monday night.

"Did you find time to meet with Zuri and Mandi?" Jack asked.

"I did, but it turned out to be a bad idea," Serena snorted. "They can't stop fighting long enough to get any information from them." *Not true. I'm sorry, Jack. You must remain clueless if my plan is to work.* She also excluded the part when Justice arrived, not wanting more questions.

As the time grew closer to Bill's arrival, Serena's nerves tingled. Her heart raced as she wondered how she would respond when their plan became a reality. She played with her teacup and pretended to listen to the conversation. Mia alone could see the entrance, and Serena instructed her to show no emotion when she saw the detective.

"Serena?" Jack called, leaning down to catch her eye. "Jun wants to know if you're finished?"

"What? Yes. Okay. Whatever." Serena forced a smile. "Sorry, I was daydreaming." She checked her watch.

"Going somewhere?" Jack asked in a teasing voice. "You have your friends and me here. What more could you want?"

"Nothing, Jack," Serena answered. "I'm happy you could join us." She placed her hand on her heart, swearing everyone could hear the loud beat. *Breath in and out, Serena. You can do this.*

"Where is she?" Bill Mitchell's booming voice bounced off the tearoom walls. "Having tea? Of course she is. A woman, who can do no wrong, is enjoying tea with friends. What a great place to arrest her."

Serena widened her eyes in mock terror. "Arrest me?" she whispered.

Bill arrived at the table with two police officers. "Serena Tate, please stand." When she did, he said, "Hands behind your back." He turned to one officer. "Cuff her."

"Wait a minute, Bill," Jack jumped from his seat. "What are you doing? Take off the cuffs."

"Recent evidence has come to light, Ando, and if you don't sit back down, I'll arrest you, too." He dangled another pair of cuffs at Jack.

Serena gave Jack a pleading look. "Do as he says, Jack."

Mia and Lily hadn't moved. They sat with shocked expressions on their faces.

"It's the best way to help her, Jack," Lily said in a quiet voice. "We can discuss strategy after they leave."

"Serena is not going to the station without me," Jack yelled. "Try to stop me."

Serena dreaded the next step in the plan. If Jack refused to back down, she had told Bill to do whatever it took.

"You're interfering with a police matter, Ando. Obstructing justice. If you don't sit down, I will arrest you. My officers will escort you straight to a cell." Bill paused for effect, then said, "How can you assist your girlfriend from jail?" He tossed in a nasty chuckle for good measure.

"Fine." Jack threw his napkin on the table and returned to his seat.

All eyes were on Serena as Bill marched her through the restaurant. She tried not to feel humiliated but couldn't shake the feeling. Bill had a tight grip on her arm as if he expected her to escape. When they reached the entrance, Serena spotted Nina rushing up the garden pathway toward the tearoom.

"I'll handle this," Serena said under her breath.

"Unhand her this minute," Nina commanded. Bill dropped his hand, and Nina took Serena aside. "One phone call, and you will be back here in no time."

"I'm under arrest, Nina. It's not that simple this time. Bill believes he has a case against me. He just received additional evidence. Enough to arrest me. Please don't do anything yet. We have nothing to go on until I discover what he has on me."

"I cannot let you leave like this," Nina cried. "The man has you in handcuffs, for goodness' sake."

"I can take care of myself," Serena whispered. "If you want to help, call your lawyer and have her on standby."

"Serena," Bill growled.

"Oh, and take care of Jack. Don't let him near the station," Serena said as Bill pulled her away from Nina. "I love you."

Serena struggled to release her arm, but Bill wouldn't budge. Once outside, she hissed, "You can let go now."

Bill removed the handcuffs and opened the front passenger side of the cruiser. He waited until Serena was comfortable before closing the door.

"I had to make it look convincing," Bill answered as he slid behind the steering wheel.

"You certainly did," Serena snarled. "Best acting performance goes to…"

"Me?" Bill chuckled.

"Did you have others arrested as well or am I the only lucky one?"

"Just you. We're bringing in your chosen three for more questioning or that's what they believe." Bill stopped at a red light. "We have a slight problem. Mr. Harrington insisted on bringing his wife to observe the procedure. I had no reason to refuse."

"It's alright, Bill. This could be beneficial." Serena paused. "Wait a minute. I take back the award, Bill. I just thought of something. You never read me my rights. I'm sure my friends are discussing it right now. Nina's lawyer will jump all over that."

"I'll say I did it before putting you in the car," Bill replied.

"This is our only chance, and I don't want it going sideways."

"Neither do I." Bill glanced at Serena. "Are you ready for what's coming?"

"Not really. We can't predict the future," Serena answered. "Let me ask you one thing while we're alone. You believe I'm innocent, right?"

Bill cleared his throat. "As much as I hate to admit it…"

"Detective." Serena interrupted. "Answer the question."

"Okay, you're innocent. Are you happy now?" Bill asked.

"Very." Serena folded her arms. "What convinced you?"

"You told me the truth, Serena. By sharing that crucial piece of evidence, you changed everything. You could have kept the contract details to yourself."

"I had no idea the document existed until Justice told me after Tasha's death."

"There's that. You learned about it after the fact." Bill nodded as he pulled into the station. "I'll need to put the cuffs on until we reach the interrogation room."

"Am I first to arrive?" Serena asked.

"As requested." Bill pressed against the door, slid out and strode around the front of the car.

An officer greeted him, and they spoke for a few minutes. Instead of Bill returning to retrieve her, the officer headed to the cruiser. "Please, come with me," he said, gesturing toward the entrance.

"Aren't you going to cuff me?" Serena asked once she stood on solid ground.

"I don't believe it's necessary," the officer answered as he led her to a room that did not resemble an interrogation room. "Detective Mitchell instructed me to leave you here."

"This isn't what I expected," Serena said.

"It's a meeting room, ma'am," the officer replied. "Choose a seat. The others should arrive shortly."

Cushioned chairs. Long table. Even a sign pointing to the bathroom. Serena ran her hand along the tabletop as she surveyed the area. Someone had placed a pitcher filled with ice water surrounded by Styrofoam cups in the middle. *I want to see the door.* She paused when she arrived at the back of the room. *Not the head of the table, though. I'll leave that for Bill.*

"Put him in conference room two."

The voice caused Serena to look up, curious to see who would enter the room. The door swung back, and they made eye contact. *Justice.*

"Hello, Serena. Fancy meeting you here." Justice's voice dripped with sarcasm.

Serena let him be angry with her. He was a pawn on her list, and she needed him at the table. "Justice." She tried to smile yet failed. "What are you doing here?"

"You know exactly why I'm here. You told Mitchell about the contract. He's arresting me for Tasha's murder."

"Is that what they told you? Did someone read you your rights?"

"Well…no." Justice rubbed his hand over his face. "They want to ask more questions. What about you?"

"Mitchell arrested me," Serena said, with no emotion. "I guess I'm the killer."

"You're not." Justice walked to where Serena sat, choosing the seat by her. "I'm sorry, baby. Here I am, blaming you for this mess, and Mitchell thinks you committed the crime."

"Funny, right?" Serena patted his hand. "You won't be here long. The detective wants to finalize this case with no glitches. He probably wants to ask a few more questions before throwing me in jail."

Chapter Eighteen

"How did we get here, Serena?" Justice asked. "A few days ago, I was going to marry Tasha, and now the police have arrested my ex-wife for her murder."

"That sounds about right," Mandi said from the open doorway. "Jeez, don't they lock prisoners up anymore?" She sauntered into the room and chose a chair across the table from them. "I don't understand why I'm here if they solved the case. I heard the police arrested you, Serena." Mandi winced. "Sorry."

"The detective probably needs to wrap up a few loose ends." Serena lifted her shoulder. "I have no idea."

"I know one thing," another woman's voice said from the entrance. "This will end today."

"Hello, Zuri," Serena said. "Welcome." *My list is complete. Bill had Zuri, Mandi and Justice brought to the station. Now all we need is for the Harrington patriarch to make his appearance. Bill had one job to do, and he better have done it.*

"You appear quite calm for someone arrested for murder," Zuri said, choosing to sit by Justice.

"I didn't do it, Zuri, and hopefully, with your help, I can prove it," Serena answered.

"Ignore her, Zuri. Don't say a word, unless they ask you a question," Justice said. "Keep your answers short and don't volunteer any information."

"Got it." Zuri nodded.

"Justice." Serena widened her eyes.

"Every man…and woman…for themselves," Justice answered.

"I never said a word about your mom," Serena said under her breath. "And she knows about the contract."

Justice flashed Serena a 'be quiet' look.

"Well?" Serena asked, hoping for a positive response.

"Okay, I'll give you that." Justice fidgeted in his chair. "What are we waiting for?"

Serena fixed her gaze on the wall clock. Each tick of the second hand seemed to drag. When fifteen minutes had passed, voices from the hallway broke the silence. Serena recognized Bill's distinctive tone, followed by the voices of another man and woman. *Mr. and Mrs. Harrington have arrived.*

Bill peeked into the room. "Yes, they are all here. We can begin. Please, after you."

Theo and Shari Harrington walked into the room, not making eye contact with anyone. Theo pulled out two chairs on Mandi's side of the table, taking the one beside her. Shari settled into the seat next to him.

Bill strode to the head of the table and appeared quite pleased with himself. "Thank you for coming today."

"We had no choice," Mandi snarled.

Bill didn't seem fazed. "I have a confession to make," he said. "One which pains me greatly. I have received some important evidence since I arrested Serena Tate. She is no longer our number one suspect." He glanced down at the table and opened the folder he'd brought with him. "You all are."

"Excuse me?" Theo Harrington sputtered. "What's the meaning of this? I came to hear the evidence which would convict that woman." He pointed across the table. "Her. She did it. It makes sense to us." He faced his wife. "Right, Shari?"

"Yes." Shari's eyes filled with tears, and she dabbed the corners with a tissue.

"Things have changed," Bill stated. He held up a paper. "This is what I received today."

Serena swore she heard Zuri gasp. *Good sign. Justice told no one.*

"What is *that*?" Theo asked.

"You should recognize it, sir. You had a contract drawn up between you and Justice Tate," Bill answered.

"I did no such thing." Theo pounded the table. "It's a forgery, I'll tell you."

"We had it verified, Mr. Harrington. It's a legal, binding contract. You signed it. Your name is on it."

"What kind of contract?" Shari asked in a weak voice.

"It's nothing, dear," Theo took Shari's hand. "Mumbo jumbo, as you like to call it. Justice signed a standard contract with the company."

"Oh." Shari sniffed.

"Do standard contracts include marriage to the owner's daughter?" Bill asked.

"That?" Theo waved his hand. "It's nothing. My lawyer asked when I wanted the contract to go into effect. I instructed him to wait until after the wedding."

"Let me see." Bill held the paper farther away from him, then finally slipped on a pair of reading glasses he kept in his shirt pocket. "After the marriage of Justice Tate to Tasha Harrington, the company will hire Justice Tate as its CEO." He made eye contact with Theo. "You are correct. It says that."

"Sounds like blackmail or a bribe to me," Serena said. She covered her mouth. "Ooh, sorry."

"What if he didn't marry your daughter, Mr. Harrington?" Bill asked.

"He wouldn't get the job," Theo mumbled.

Bill returned to the document. "You signed this contract." He pointed to the spot. "As did Mr. Tate."

"May I?" Serena held up her hand.

"Keep it short," Bill snarled.

"Mr. Harrington, if you had your lawyer write in one more sentence, we might not be here today," Serena said.

"And what is that?" Theo barked.

"If for any reason, the wedding does not take place, this contract is void." Serena puckered her lips. "But you didn't add that one simple sentence. After Tasha's death, you couldn't tear up your contract and pretend it didn't exist. Justice still had his copy. Perhaps he might use it to sue you or prove he planned to marry Tasha, and her untimely death prohibited it from happening. He might try to claim his job. Not what you wanted, was it, Mr. Harrington?"

"What are you saying?" Theo leaned over the table as if he wanted to throttle Serena. "You think I killed my daughter to get out some darn contract?"

"I don't think you killed your daughter, sir. You hired someone to dust the bouquet, and this person used too much peanut butter powder," Serena answered.

"I did what?"

"Did you pay Jacqui Greene to do the job?" Serena asked, unfazed by Harrington's attitude.

"I'll take it from here," Bill said. He faced Theo. "Please answer the question, Mr. Harrington."

"I'm not saying another word until I call my lawyer," Theo answered.

"I'll have an officer take you into the hallway to make your call," Bill said. "But let me remind you that you are not a suspect or under arrest. Do you really want to bring in legal counsel?"

"No, I want you to solve this case."

"Then let me." Bill folded his arms and waited. "Well?"

"I never hired Jacqui Greene or anyone else to taint the bouquet," Theo said in a defeated voice.

"Okay," Bill said, turning to Zuri. "Justice said you knew about the contract."

"I did not!" Justice yelled.

"Ms. Brooks, please answer the question." Bill focused all his attention on her.

"Okay." Zuri held up her hands. "I knew."

"Before the wedding or after?"

"Before," Zuri said in a meek voice.

"Are you in love with Justice Tate?" Bill asked.

"How does that relate to this case?" Justice cried.

"Justice." Serena placed her hand on his arm. "Stay out of this. Let Zuri answer."

"Yes," Zuri whispered.

"Would you do anything for him?" Bill asked.

"Yes."

* * * *

Bill called for a recess, allowing everyone but Serena to leave the room. "You are still under arrest," he informed her in front of the others. "We'll reconvene in thirty minutes." He waited until they were alone and asked. "What's your take?"

"You called a recess so we could discuss the case?" Serena asked. "You want my opinion?"

"I do." Bill nodded.

"Zuri sounds guilty, but we know she is innocent. You turned to her because Theo threatened to call his lawyer, which would have shut down this investigation."

"Exactly. The man is hiding something, Serena. I feel it in my bones."

Serena lifted a brow. "How do we get him to talk?"

"We have found that the longer we keep people here, someone eventually breaks down. I've watched Mrs. Harrington, looking for any signs of guilt or knowledge of the crime, but I truly believe she is here for the right reason. She wants her daughter's killer found."

"Mandi has stayed pretty quiet, and that's unusual for her."

"She wants to keep under the radar," Bill replied. "If she speaks, I may start asking her questions."

"Then maybe we should question her. I'll ask if she has anything to add to the conversation," Serena suggested.

"You can, but remember, this is my case. My arrest."

"Bill." Serena narrowed her eyes. "They are always your cases and your arrests. Why can't you accept I'm trying to help?" She gestured to the restroom sign. "If you don't mind?"

"Sure." Bill stood and exited the room.

Upon her return from the restroom, Serena was surprised to find a glass of iced tea and a sandwich waiting for her. She hadn't thought about eating, but the food looked tempting. *Everyone else is eating. Why not me?*

As Serena chewed her sandwich, she reviewed and analyzed what people had said. *I removed Zuri from my list, and it will stay that way. We are down to two people. Theo and Mandi. I think Mandi is enjoying the show with no need to defend herself. Well, Ms. Amanda Shaw, it's your turn. Time to answer some questions.*

The door opened to expose Nina and Bill in the hallway. An officer held it back as they entered. Nina wore a determined expression, and Serena realized nothing would stop her.

"I will have you out of here within the hour, Serena," Nina said.

Serena met Bill's eyes. "Can I speak with her privately?"

"Of course."

"Nina, please sit." Serena pulled out a chair and sat beside her. *I must tell her the truth.* "I need to stay here. Bill and I are working together."

"You and Bill?" Nina's eyes widened.

"Yes, it took some convincing, but he agreed to work with me. I'm sorry I didn't tell you, but I needed authentic reactions from you and Jack." Serena explained the plan, condensing it for time.

"I understand completely." Nina took Serena's hand. "I will act as if I am outraged over the situation and leave."

"Thanks." Serena squeezed Nina's hand. "Please update Jack. I don't want him storming in here."

"Is that what I did?" Nina teased.

"Oh, Nina, of course you did. Don't you know? You are a force of nature." Serena laughed.

"How is everything in here?" Bill asked, standing in the entryway. "I'm sorry, but I must ask you to leave, Mrs. Takeda. Time's up. People will return in five minutes, and it's best that they don't see you."

"If I must." Nina exhaled, then smiled. "Keep up the good work, Detective. Your plan is quite impressive."

Serena watched an officer lead Nina away in another direction. "Smart. She shouldn't be seen by the others," she said.

"Yes," Bill answered. "Luckily, Mrs. Takeda is a reasonable woman."

"Until you cross her," Serena kidded.

"Is that a…" Bill pointed at her.

"Joke? Yes, Bill, it's called a joke." Serena grinned. "Did our suspects leave the building for lunch?"

"No, but we let them order food through a service," Bill answered. "I don't want anyone to say I prohibited them from eating or drinking." He gestured over his shoulder towards a drink station. "Coffee?"

"Police station coffee?" Serena asked. "Is that anything like hospital coffee?"

"Probably worse."

"Now that's a good joke," Serena chuckled. "I'll just have some ice water." Serena tilted her head, listening for voices. "Are they coming? I don't hear anything."

"No, I doubt if they'll return until the half hour is up. Did you think of something?"

"Yes, we need to focus on Mandi when everyone returns. If we get nothing from her, it's back to Theo. We'll keep asking them questions until someone breaks…like you said."

"I like the way you think." Bill walked to the door and leaned into the hallway. "They're coming."

★ ★ ★ ★

The remaining suspects entered as a group, returning to the same seats. After Justice slid into his, he asked, "Did you eat, Serena? I can't believe Mitchell kept you in here."

"Are you worried about me, Justice?" Serena fluttered her lashes and touched her throat. "I didn't know you cared."

"I care," Justice huffed. "I'm angry at you, but I'll get over it."

"You may get over it sooner than you think," Serena said. "And, yes, I ate. Someone brought me an iced tea and a turkey sandwich." She held up the half-full plastic cup and jiggled it, making the cubes swirl in the liquid. "See?"

"I don't get it, Serena. Why are you so calm? I expected you to try harder to vindicate yourself."

"Oh, believe me, Justice. I am trying." Serena winked. She looked at Mandi, who appeared relaxed as she chatted with the Harringtons. For some reason, it made her blood boil. "Mandi, what are your thoughts on these proceedings? You've said little, and the detective hasn't asked you any questions. Don't you find it strange?"

"No, I don't, Serena. I'm sure they brought me in as a witness, nothing else. I was Tasha's best friend and will correct any lies told about her. There's no reason to question me again."

"That's quite a friend," Serena said. "If you knew the contract existed, would you have informed Tasha?"

"And break her heart?" Mandi cried. "No way. Besides, I never knew about a contract. Justice only confides in her." She gestured at Zuri.

Serena felt Mandi was trying to remove the spotlight from herself and place it elsewhere. Starting a fight with Zuri would do the trick. Unwilling to referee again, Serena glanced at Bill, who stood at the head of the table. He gave her a slight nod, indicating he would take over.

"Thank you for returning on time," Bill said. "Now let's get down to business. No one leaves this room until I get some answers."

Chapter Nineteen

"You can't force us to stay here against our will," Theo shouted.

"If I believe you are suspects, I can," Bill answered.

"You already arrested the culprit." Theo pointed at Serena. "Be done with it, Mitchell," he growled.

"As I said before, Mr. Harrington, Ms. Tate is no longer under arrest. This document reached my desk after I brought her to the station." He waved the paper in the air. "It's the reason you are here."

"I think you protest too much, Mr. Harrington," Serena said with fire in her voice. "You want this over and don't care who is guilty as long as it's not *you*."

"That's a ridiculous accusation," Theo snorted. "I will admit to having my lawyer draw up the contract, and I signed it. I have nothing to hide."

"Did you change your mind about hiring Justice?" Serena asked. "You haven't answered that question. The week of the wedding, the marriage between Tasha and Justice became real, didn't it? Once Tasha married Justice, he would become CEO of a company you founded. He wasn't your employee and didn't start in the filing room like many of your executives. It grated on your nerves the more you thought about it."

"Fine. Yes. It got to me." Theo hung his head. "It was too late to do anything."

"Except stop the wedding," Bill said. "It would give you time to nullify the contract."

"Yes," Theo whispered.

"Yet, Theo was nowhere near the floral shop," Serena said. "He must have hired someone or…" She zoned in on Mandi. "found a willing accomplice. Someone who needed money. Did Tasha threaten to end your agreement, Mandi? Stop giving you handouts?"

"No, Serena. Tasha never gave me money." Mandi widened her eyes and cocked her head at the Harringtons.

"Oh, that's right. You don't want them to know." Serena nodded. "Got it. But extra cash wouldn't hurt, would it?" She paused. "I can picture it now. Theo appeared upset, and being Tasha's closest friend, you approached him to ask why. Once Theo confided in you, you agreed to help him. Both of you were aware of Tasha's allergy. When did Theo confide in you, Mandi?"

"We spoke the night before the rehearsal dinner. Tasha hosted a happy hour for the bridal party, hoping we would bond." She snickered. "She wanted this cohesive group of friends, cheering for her and Justice."

Mandi spoke the truth. Serena recalled Jade and Jewel going out that evening and promising not to drink. "You and Theo talked about stopping the wedding that night.

Whose idea was it to sprinkle powder on the bouquet? Was it you, Mandi?" she asked.

Tears welled in Mandi's eyes. "No," she whispered.

"Stop harassing the poor woman," Theo yelled. "Don't you see she's upset?" He placed his arm around her.

Surprised by his actions, Serena glanced at Bill. He nodded for her to keep going. "You were alone in the back room of the flower shop, Mandi," she said. "Jacqui can testify to it."

"The lab did not find your fingerprints on the box, Ms. Shaw, however, we possess evidence confirming your presence in the room." Bill opened his folder. "Let's see here. Amanda Shaw. Yes, your name is on the list of prints found at the floral shop."

"What parts of the shop?" Serena asked.

"Countertop. Door handle." Bill closed the folder. "Ms. Shaw, did Theo Harrington ask you to apply the powder to the bouquet?"

"I would never do that!" Theo roared. "Mandi and I discussed a few ways we could stop the wedding. They were all hypothetical."

"He's right," Mandi shouted. "Leave him…and me… alone."

"Mandi," Theo took her hand. "Tasha had a serious allergy to peanuts. Her mother and I watched what she ate ever since she was diagnosed as a child. We reminded her constantly to be careful. You would never jeopardize her life. Am I right?"

"I wouldn't." Mandi grasped her bottom lip between her teeth. "Yet, you said if you had a way, you'd dose her bouquet."

"It was a joke!" Theo threw his hand in the air.

"You were so desperate, Theo," Mandi cried.

"Did you do something?" Theo roared.

"I wanted to help you. Take away your pain."

"And?" Theo grabbed Mandi's upper arm. "You went to the floral shop and dosed the bouquet with peanut butter powder?" he asked.

Mandi dropped her head and whispered. "Yes."

"What did you say? I didn't hear you," Theo growled.

"I only meant to sprinkle a little powder on the bouquet. My hand slipped. Before I could remove the excess, Jacqui entered the room. She closed the box and sealed it. 'You're my witness,' she said. 'The bride will be the next person to open the box.'"

Serena smiled at Bill, closing and opening her eyes as she tilted her head at Mandi. "Now's your chance," she whispered.

"Amanda Shaw," Bill said. "You are under arrest for the murder of Tasha Harrington." He made eye contact with a guard posted at the door. "Cuff her."

"No! Wait." Shari pushed back her chair and stood. Placing her hands on the table, she leaned forward to gaze at Mandi. "I want to know why you would help my husband, *Amanda*. Start talking."

"Oh," Serena whispered. *Shari figured it out before I did.*

Past conversations with Mandi flooded Serena's mind. *Tasha and Mandi's girl code. Don't tell anyone about the money.* She massaged her temple, trying to put it all together. *Mandi used Tasha as a cover. She didn't get the money from Tasha. Mandi received payments from the man himself, Theo Harrington.*

"Mrs. Harrington, we need to…" Bill replied.

"If you have any sympathy for a grieving mother, you will give me this moment, Detective," Shari interrupted with a stern voice. "I'd like to hear Mandi's story. *All* of it."

Mandi began to weep, and Theo pulled her closer. "Hasn't she been through enough?" he demanded.

"I haven't even started, Theo," Shari snarled. "Stop crying, *Amanda*, and start talking."

Mandi pulled away from Theo, sat up in her chair and sniffed. "While I was going through my divorce, I often visited Tasha at your house." She looked over at Shari. "Tasha was having work done at her home and moved in with you until the workers finished. One day, when I needed her most, she wasn't there. Theo invited me in, offered me a drink and let me talk. He was so kind and caring."

"That's when you started the affair," Serena said with confidence. "Theo gave you the money, not Tasha."

"You make it sound cold, Serena. It wasn't like that. I love Theo. He wanted to help me."

"Love?" Shari yelled. "You called me 'Mom' when you visited my home, but you really came to see Theo. How could I be so stupid?"

Theo turned to her. "You're not stupid, Shari. I'm sorry. It just happened."

"It just *happened*? Do you love her?" Shari pointed a shaky finger at Mandi.

"I care about her," Theo said.

"Did you hear that, Mandi?" Shari yelled. "He said, 'Care,' not love. You're just another silly little homewrecker."

Mandi sobbed into her hands. "I'm sorry."

"Is the affair the reason Tasha ended your friendship?" Serena asked.

"She suspected something. Tasha saw me pull out of her parents' driveway as she was arriving home. She thought it was strange and confronted me. I never told her, Theo." Mandi grabbed his arm. "I swear. She figured it out on her own."

"Am I allowed to speak?" Zuri asked. "I would like to ask Mandi a question."

"Go ahead." Bill nodded with a wry smile.

"Why did you reach out to Tasha last year? You said you wanted to mend your friendship. Was that a lie?"

"Not really. Theo asked me to contact her and repair our friendship," Mandi replied. "He didn't like that Tasha had started seeing Justice again. Their dates were happening more frequently. Theo thought I could keep watch and warn him if something went amiss."

"So, you were a spy," Zuri said, her voice dripping with sarcasm. "You didn't care about Tasha's friendship at all.

Congratulations, though. You did such an excellent job, Tasha asked you to be maid of honor."

"I cared about her," Mandi whispered.

"But you wanted to keep Theo happy. You did it for him," Serena said. "Such a busy girl, Mandi. How did you manage it all?"

"I didn't mean to hurt anyone," Mandi cried. "You believe me, don't you, Theo?"

Reality appeared to have set in, and Theo grasped Mandi by the chin, holding it tightly. "I do, but you need to pay for what you've done," he growled.

"Will you help me?" Mandi's bottom lip quivered. She didn't appear to be afraid of his angry demeanor.

"Help you? After what you've done?" Theo widened his eyes and shook his head.

Serena caught Bill's eye. "Can they charge her with premeditated murder?" she asked in a quiet voice.

"It's up to the D.A., Serena, but this crime certainly qualifies. She planned the deed in advance, and there was purpose behind it. But a lawyer may argue Mandi did not research and plan the crime to that extent. She made a spontaneous decision. Her intent was to stop the wedding, not kill the bride."

A wave of sadness swept through Serena. *If only this had a different ending.* She looked across the table and saw Theo Harrington still speaking with Mandi, not comforting his wife. *If he's in Mandi's corner, perhaps they'll convict her of a lesser crime.*

Shari gathered her things and turned to Theo. "Coming?" Her voice sounded bitter, disillusioned.

"Send the car back for me," Theo replied. "I want to speak to the detective before I leave."

"Fine. Have it your way. You always do." Shari tossed her head and strode from the room.

"The rest of you are free to go," Bill said. "Serena, Justice, Zuri, thank you for your time."

"Wait," Serena said. "Before I leave, I want to ask Mandi a question."

"Sure." Bill shrugged.

"At the rehearsal, you acted as if your world had ended because Justice was marrying Tasha. You said he was the love of your life."

"I had to make it believable," Mandi replied. "Everyone expected me to fall apart at the wedding. I didn't care if he married Tasha," she huffed. "Or anyone else, for that matter. Even you, Zuri," she snarled. "When I made that speech, I meant it. Tasha was a lucky girl. Justice is a catch. But I love Theo. I did it for him."

"Thanks for giving a truthful answer," Serena replied. She turned to Justice and Zuri and gave them a nod. "We should go."

The three rose from their chairs, and Bill followed them. "Oh, Ms. Tate. I have some papers for you to sign," he said.

Serena spun on her heels and narrowed her eyes. "Papers?"

Bill gestured down the hallway. "Could you please come this way?" Once Serena joined him, he said, "I wanted to thank you. We made an effective team. Ever think of joining the force?"

"Never." Serena gave him a deadpan expression.

"This isn't the outcome Theo Harrington wanted, but he got his answer." Bill hung his head. "Very sad. His daughter died because of his need to control, a stupid contract and his infidelity."

"True," Serena answered. "But we solved the mystery, Bill."

"Serena!" Jack rushed up to her, taking her hands in his. "Is Mitchell harassing you?"

"Quite the opposite, Jack." Serena chuckled. "He offered me a job."

* * * *

"Mom!" Serena's girls rushed into her open arms.

"Are you okay?" Jade asked.

"We were so worried," Jewel said. "You were gone forever."

"Forever is a long time, sweetie," Serena said, kissing Jewel's forehead. "But we cracked the case."

"Who did it?" Lily held up her hands with palms together, begging for an answer.

"Let Serena breathe," Nina said, ushering everyone away from Serena. "She just walked into the hotel. Why don't we continue our discussion in the tearoom?"

"We ordered all your favorites," Mia replied. "Almond cookies, oolong tea, scones…"

"Sounds wonderful," Serena answered and slipped her hand into Jack's. "I'm sorry," she said as they walked along the flagstone pathway.

"For what?" Jack wrinkled his nose.

"Keeping you in the dark."

"It's okay." Jack squeezed her hand. "Besides, don't you know your friends by now? To keep me from leaving the hotel, they had to tell me the truth. I would never let you be alone at the station."

"Bill would have denied you access and barred you from the room."

"I would have sat in the hallway." Jack grinned. "Since Nina wanted to check on you, we voted she should go to the station and insist on seeing you. I texted Sue and asked her to let me know when Bill called a recess."

"Sue helped?" Serena's heart burst with love and happiness. She hadn't been alone the entire time she sat in the interrogation room. "They say raising a child requires a village, but no matter how old we get, we need one. Thank you, everyone."

Once settled at the table, Jun appeared with tea, followed by another server who carried the cookies and scones. "Thanks, Mori," she nodded as she dismissed the teen. Jun's eyes widened as she looked at Serena and said, "We are alone now. Please tell us, Serena. Who did it?"

Jun appeared so serious, no one dared crack a smile. "Well, Jun," Serena answered. "And everyone else…it was Mandi."

"I knew it!" Jun grinned and left the table.

"I never would have guessed," Jewel said, making eye contact with her sister. "Did you think Mandi did it?"

"Mandi kept talking about this mystery boyfriend, and it wasn't Dad," Jade answered. "Because of that, I never expected her to kill Tasha." She glanced at Serena. "Did you uncover the mystery man's identity? Mandi's actual boyfriend?"

"Oh, we certainly did." Serena hesitated, letting the suspense build. "Theo Harrington," she said with gusto. "Can you believe it?" Everyone appeared shocked, except Nina. "Nina, what are you thinking?"

"Never underestimate anyone, Serena. We've always said people do things for revenge, power, money or love. It seems our Ms. Shaw thought she would prove her love in quite the drastic fashion."

"Funny thing, it may have worked," Serena replied. "Theo stayed behind to speak with Bill Mitchell. He didn't go storming out of the room with his wife."

"Do you think he will stand by Mandi?" Lily asked.

"We'll have to wait and see," Serena answered.

Chapter Twenty

"The summer has passed by so quickly, Jack," Serena said as they strolled through the gardens. "It's already the end of August."

"It has indeed," Jack answered. "Tasha's murder case took up a lot of our time. I'm glad Mandi agreed to plead guilty once they settled on involuntary manslaughter."

"If I remember correctly," Serena said. "Manslaughter is when someone kills without premeditation or malicious intent."

"Correct," Jack replied. "The killing happens because of recklessness, negligence or in the heat of passion. Mandi could receive a five-to-ten-year sentence."

"I wonder if Theo will wait for her or has gone back to his wife."

"I'd wait for you." Jack pulled her close when they reached the pond. "Luckily, that didn't happen."

"Don't even joke about it, Jack." Serena kissed him and from the corner of her eye, she spotted Samurai. "He's here," she whispered.

"You said he agreed to meet me," Jack said under his breath. "Is it time?"

Serena stepped up to the railing. "Samurai, I want you to meet Jack. He came here seeking help when the police arrested me and tried to talk to you. I never made a formal introduction, which may explain why you stayed away. But today's the day, Sam. Come and meet, Jack."

A red head finally emerged from the water. Sam swam to the edge of the pond and grinned at Serena. "You little stinker." She laughed. "Are you jealous of Jack?'

Sam dove into the water and popped up his head, then swam in a circle and lifted his tail. Serena giggled at his actions. "Yes, and no. He can't decide, Jack."

"Can I speak with Sam alone?" Jack asked.

"Sure. I'll visit the shrine so you two can talk."

Serena followed the walkway which led to Kaito Masuda's shrine. Two lion-dog stone statues stood guard on either side of the three-foot high stone wall entrance. A sign urged respectful decorum before stepping into the sanctuary. Decorative before Nina's brother died, the shrine now held Kaito's ashes. Serena glanced up at the security camera, which she knew someone always monitored. *Nina Takeda doesn't take chances with her brother.*

"Hey, Kaito." Serena waved as she stepped into the sacred space. "I needed a peaceful moment and knew I would find it here. I'm sure you've heard many random stories from The Pearl's guests, but you hold a special place in my heart as does your sister."

When Serena first met her, Nina had revealed the history of The Pearl hotel and its gardens over tea. She and her brother Kaito had nurtured a dream of building a hotel since childhood. Three decades ago, their youthful aspirations transformed into a remarkable reality. Amidst the bustling construction phase, Kaito had brought a sketchpad and colored pencils to the site. With his eye for design, he drew as he spoke about the possibilities for the gardens, producing wonderful pictures from his words. His creative side always amazed his sister, while her organizational and analytic skills awed him. They worked well together and dreamed of crafting a space which would captivate any visitor, hoping guests would return when in the city. Their dreams came to fruition, and The Pearl was highly regarded.

"But first it takes a vision," Serena whispered. "You were the visionary, Kaito. Nina always gives you credit." She folded her hands. "She misses you terribly."

"Speaking with my brother?" Nina's voice floated towards Serena.

"Nina." Serena turned to face her and smiled. "I speak to Kaito from time to time. There's a sense of calm and tranquility here. The longer I stay, my mind becomes unburdened, and the serene atmosphere soothes the soul."

"Quite profound." Nina nodded. "I hope others get that feeling when they stop to visit or even pass by. Kaito still keeps giving, even in death." A single tear rolled down Nina's cheek.

"Oh, Nina, I didn't mean to make you sad," Serena said in a worried voice.

"You didn't, my dear child. I love when you ask about Kaito. It is always a joy to speak of him. Many people avoid the subject, thinking it would bring me pain, but it is just the opposite. He died too young and keeping his memory alive is important to me."

"Okay, then I'll keep asking a million questions," Serena teased, hoping Nina would take it the right way.

"I know you will." Nina smiled. "I believe Jack is waiting for you by the pond, Serena."

"How did you…" Serena waved her hand. "After I finished my visit with Kaito, I planned to return to the pond. Jack finally met Samurai. Can you believe it?"

"Samurai always waits for the right moment, Serena. Never doubt him," Nina replied.

"Jack wanted to speak with Sam in private." Serena chuckled. "I think I gave them enough time."

"If you are available later, would you and Jack join me for dinner?" Nina asked.

"We would love to. Dining room?"

"Yes, please arrive at seven. Now, if you will excuse me, I must get back to work."

Serena pulled her brows together as she watched Nina leave the gardens. *That was strange. Nina found me and sent me to the pond. She doesn't follow my every move here…or does she?*

When Serena arrived at the pond, she discovered Jack waiting on the bench, lost in thought. "Hey." She slid onto the seat and cuddled up to him, wrapping her hands around his upper arm. "This is nice."

"Doing nothing?" Jack asked. "I agree." He inhaled and gradually let out the breath. "Serena, is this truly your favorite place? You don't have another? Perhaps one you haven't told me about."

"Jack, my appreciation for this place has grown since the police almost arrested me for murder. I believe I took things for granted. Now, when I walk through the gardens, I study a single flower or a stone pagoda, to ensure nothing is missed. When I first arrived at The Pearl, the gardens melded into one big, beautiful space. Now, I see it as separate, unique parts coming together to create this wonderful paradise. Does that make sense?" Serena leaned back and gazed at the ceiling. Sun rays poured through the skylights, illuminating the space with a natural brilliance. Every shadow and every shimmer felt alive.

"Yes, it does. I love it here, too."

When she lowered her gaze to look at the pond, Serena found Jack on one knee in front of her. "Jack!" she gasped.

"Serena Baker Tate, I love you. I can't say it enough. I can't show you enough. You are my everything. Our first meeting ignited a spark, and I felt an immediate connection." Jack paused. "Even though I was guarding the models' dressing room, and you were trying to sneak in." He grinned.

"I had permission," Serena protested.

"Debatable," Jack chuckled, then held up his hand. "May I continue?"

"Certainly." Tears filled Serena's eyes. Her heart felt so full she thought it would burst. Whatever Jack said next, she already knew the answer.

"I've spoken with Robin and Samurai. Both have given me permission to ask this question." Jack pressed his lips together. "Serena Elizabeth, will you marry me?"

"Yes, Jack Ando, I will marry you." Serena bounced up from the bench. "I will be Serena Baker Tate Ando. Well, forget the Tate. Do the girls know? How did I not see this coming?"

"Serena." Jack stood and placed his hands on her shoulders. "Take a calming breath. Please, look at the pond."

Sam's head poked out of the water. He dove deep into the pond and returned with a chorus of fish. Serena gasped at the sight of the colorful koi, all coming to congratulate her. "Thank you, Sam," she whispered.

Jack held a black velvet box in his hand and lifted the top. "I hope it fits," he said as only Jack could.

"It will." Serena let him slide the princess cut diamond with a double-wide band of tiny ones onto her finger. "See." She held out her hand to admire it. "Perfect." Serena looked over her shoulder. "I'm surprised my entire family hasn't jumped out of the bushes."

"Only Robin knows," Jack answered. "I swore her to secrecy."

"And Nina." Serena gave him a knowing look.

"And Nina." Jack smiled. "May I kiss my fiancée?"

"Ooh. I like the sound of it. Fiancée." Serena melted into Jack's arms, maintaining eye contact. She felt a powerful connection between them. "Yes, I will marry you," she whispered, wanting to say the words again.

Joy and excitement filled the surrounding space. A new life chapter was about to begin.

"I can't wait to make you my wife," Jack said, his voice shaking with emotion.

"And I can't wait to call you my husband." Serena gave Jack a kiss to remember, full of tenderness and love. One that said this was the start of a wonderful life.

* * * *

Serena chose a black cocktail dress from her closet. The sleeveless, fit-and-flare style felt right for the occasion. Heading into the bathroom, she opened her makeup drawer. "I need a bold nighttime look," she said to the mirror. "I better hurry. Jack will be here any minute."

As she searched for a pair of black heels, Serena heard a knock, and Jack's voice. "Serena?"

"Bedroom closet," Serena answered. "I'm looking for a pair of shoes. Ooh. Found them." She grabbed the heels and went out to the sitting room. "Jack," she exclaimed. "You look so handsome."

Used to seeing him in various solid-colored t-shirts and jeans, Serena realized he actually had great fashion sense. Under his fitted dark gray suit jacket, he wore a light gray dress shirt, opened at the collar. Slim-fit dress pants finished the look.

Jack held up a long, black velvet box. "For you. An engagement present."

"No, you just gave me this gorgeous ring. It's too much."

"Serena," Jack said. "You know you want to open it."

"Okay. I do." Serena smiled. "Ooh, I must practice saying that for our wedding day." She took the box and popped the lid. "Oh, my, it's beautiful!" A long string of tiny diamonds glistened against the black velvet. "Thank you, Jack. Will you help me put it on?"

Jack took the choker necklace from the box and placed it around Serena's neck. It went perfectly with the V-neck of her dress. He kissed her shoulder after he snapped the clasp shut. "The necklace looks like it was designed for you." He guided her to the mirror by the front door. "See?"

Serena studied her reflection. Her curly hair skimmed along her shoulders as she turned to admire the jewelry. She felt the soft locks brush against her skin. "I could get used to this, Jack." She touched the necklace.

"I did well?" Jack asked.

"Yes, but I'd love anything you'd give me." Serena checked how the necklace looked in the mirror. "Are these real?" She teased.

"Of course." Jack stood behind her and looked into the mirror. "We make quite the pair."

"Hmm, that's what Bill Mitchell recently said to me," Serena replied with a nudge to his ribs.

"Not as detectives, Serena," Jack said, pretending to be annoyed. "As partners in life."

Serena turned to face him. "I knew it from the moment I first saw you, Jack. We were meant to be."

"It was quite the meeting." Jack chuckled. "And it has been a roller coaster ride ever since."

"The ride has stopped, Jack. Look where we ended up." Serena placed her lips against Jack's. She gently kissed him and felt his arms go around her. "This is where I want to be," she whispered in between kisses.

"Me, too. What if we skipped dinner?" Jack asked.

"Nina would kill us."

"She wouldn't."

"Probably would."

"Okay, maybe," Jack said. "Let's go."

Chapter Twenty One

The maître d' escorted Jack and Serena to the private dining room. Serena tugged on Jack's hand and said, "Something is up. I can feel it."

"We'll soon find out," Jack answered.

"Surprise!" a chorus of voices greeted them.

Nina rose from her seat and approached the couple. "Congratulations," she said. "It was spur-of-the-moment, but I invited your friends and family for an informal engagement party. I hope it is alright."

Serena's eyes welled with tears as she took in the room, her heart swelling at the sight of her loved ones gathered for this special occasion. Mia and Kade sat with Lily and Gabe at a table joined by Kal, Nina's husband. Her girls had their boyfriends, Andre and Carmody, by their sides. Robin caught her eye and waved from her seat, gesturing toward two empty seats. Everyone who mattered most came to celebrate the engagement, filling the space with warmth and love. "What more could a girl want?" Serena whispered.

"Then let the celebration begin," Nina exclaimed. "A champagne toast is required." She leaned in and said only to Serena, "Sparkling juice for the girls."

"Thank you," Serena said. "I know they can't wait until they turn twenty-one, but I'd like to keep them nineteen a little longer."

Jack cleared his throat.

"What?" Serena turned to him.

"One glass won't hurt. I'm sure it isn't their first drink."

"Jack Ando." Serena placed her hand on her hip. "Siding with the girls against me?" She teased.

"Never." Jack kissed Serena's cheek. "I'm always on your side. Your decision."

"Okay." Serena nodded. "Nina, please tell the servers the girls may have half a glass of champagne. Now that's settled, I want to hug everyone."

Making the rounds with Jack, Serena proudly showed Mia and Lily her ring. They made the appropriate comments, although Serena knew their rings were twice the size. She loved her friends' nonjudgemental nature, and the feeling extended to everyone in the room.

Serena and Jack settled in at their table, savoring the warm and inviting atmosphere as they enjoyed their meal. The Steak Oscar, tender and cooked to perfection, was topped with luscious crab and hollandaise and served with seasoned fresh vegetables. Every bite was a delight, adding to the magic of the evening.

"Mom," Jade said. "Now that we've finished dinner, can we discuss the wedding? Have you picked a date?"

"Jade, I just got engaged a few hours ago." Serena laughed. "So, no, I haven't even considered it."

"Jewel and I already decided that you should not get married in June," Jade replied.

"Due to recent circumstances, I understand," Serena answered. "June is out."

"We don't want you to wait forever," Jewel said. "But could you choose a time that doesn't coincide with school or finals?"

"I think we can accommodate your schedules," Jack said. "Which means July or August?"

"Or…" Jewel held up her pointer finger. "A Christmas wedding. Think about it. Aunt Sasha promised to come for the holidays again. She could attend the wedding, too."

"The girl makes sense, Serena," Robin replied.

"It only gives me four months to plan," Serena answered. "I'm not sure."

"Mom." Jade locked eyes with her. "Didn't you recently tell me we have a village to help us? Look around. Your village is here."

"Yes, Jade," Serena said. "You're definitely right." She turned to Jack. "Although I believe Jack has a say in the matter."

"I would like to confirm with my family before you start the arrangements," Jack said. "Other than that, I'm fine with letting you and the girls plan the wedding."

"You're not getting off that easy." Serena chuckled. "You will be involved."

"I'd like to ask my brother to be my best man, Serena," Jack said in a voice only she could hear.

"Ooh, I didn't even think of who I'd have in the bridal party besides the girls. I can't choose one over the other for maid of honor." Serena tapped the table. "I'd love to ask Mia, but it might hurt Lily's feelings."

Jack gave her a look that said he had the answer. "Ask Sasha."

"My cousin? Can I count on her to come?" Serena paused to think.

Sasha Robinson, three years younger than Serena, had wanderlust since she could talk. Serena recalled her pointing to pictures of the Taj Mahal, the Eiffel Tower and Niagara Falls, saying she wanted to go there. Sasha never chose amusement parks or water parks, like Serena did. She wanted to see the world.

Serena thought back to a conversation she had with her mom last year. Robin had brought up Sasha, reminding Serena of their childhood bond, but after an art scholarship took Sasha to Paris, it became her permanent home. The family rarely saw her.

"My cousin always followed her own path, Mama." Serena had told her. "When Sasha got the offer to study art in Paris, she couldn't turn it down. She had talent. I encouraged her to go. So did you."

"I thought she'd come back, Serena. Not stay there forever." Robin hung her head. "Sasha barely calls or texts her parents or me besides the obligatory holiday and birthday cards."

"Lovingly hand painted and created by her. She makes her living as a watercolorist. Cards, small florals, garden paintings and beautiful landmark images, to name a few," Serena replied. "Her life is there. She made a name for herself in Europe, and it has become her career. We need to accept her choice and wish her well. I can't fault Sasha for following her dream, but I wish she'd come home more often."

"More often?" Serena remembered her mom's hurt expression. "She came once for your father's funeral and when your aunt and uncle moved to Nevada."

"That's part of your problem, Mama. You miss your brother," Serena had stated. "Uncle Damian and you were close."

"Like you and Sasha," Robin replied. "She was closer to being a sister than a cousin. You called each other Sissy. Once she left, our family fell apart. Dad died, my brother moved to another state, and you divorced Justice."

"Mama, it's not that bad. Plus, Sasha left when she was nineteen. Those other things happened much later. Stop putting the blame on her."

Serena sighed. *Has it been almost a year since we had that conversation?*

"Serena?" Jack touched her arm. "What are you thinking?"

"I'm going to call my cousin as soon as we pick a date and tell her to book a plane ticket home."

"Okay, best man and maid of honor problem is solved. Jade and Jewel can be your bridesmaids."

"Who will be your groomsmen?" Serena wrinkled her brow.

"You've already met one. Tiger Wilson."

"Ooh, that handsome, fit Black man who worked on some cases with us?" Serena waved her hand in front of her face.

"Yes." Jack smirked. "The other is Doc McIntire. He makes up part of our team when we go on missions."

"Missions." Serena gazed at him. "Like Mission Impossible. I knew it."

"Hey," Jewel said. "We've given you two enough time to talk. Have you made any decisions?"

"Yes," Serena answered. "We elected to have a Christmas wedding, as long as Jack's family agrees, and have chosen our wedding party."

"Wow!" Jade exclaimed. "I'm impressed. Tell us. Are we in it?" She gestured to Jewel and herself.

"You're seriously asking that question? Of course you are," Serena said. She noticed Jewel scrolling on her phone. "Jewel, can you please put that away during my party?"

"Mom." Jewel glanced up and gave her an exasperated look. "I'm searching for Christmas wedding ideas."

"That's sweet, but it can wait," Serena replied.

"Serena." Jack nudged her. "Look."

Serena turned away from Jewel and glanced in the direction Jack pointed. Justice stood in the entryway, looking like a model in his designer suit. He had not come alone. Zuri had her hand wrapped around his upper arm as if she needed support. "Are we allowed to come in?" he asked, appearing contrite for once in his life.

"Mom," Jade said. "Jewel and I invited him. It's time we acknowledge Dad is a part of our lives. *All* of our lives."

Jack hopped from his seat and approached the couple. "Justice, good to see you." He extended his hand.

"I hear congratulations are in order," Justice said, taking Jack's hand.

"Zuri, you look lovely." Jack nodded at her.

Zuri wore a light blue sleeveless cocktail dress, which hugged her petite frame. "Thanks," she replied in a soft voice, gazing at the floor.

"I agree with Jack," Serena said, joining the group. "Please, won't you sit?"

"We just stopped by to say congratulations, "Justice said. "I made a dinner reservation in the main dining room."

"Nonsense," Nina replied as she approached them. "Serena, show your guests to that empty table. I will inform the chef to prepare two more dinners."

Serena walked to the table, followed by Jack, Justice and Zuri. She sat down, signaling Jack to join her. "We'll visit until your food arrives," she said.

"I can tell by that look in your eye that we won't be making small talk." Justice winked.

"No, we won't." Serena tried to remain serious but smiled. "I have a few questions." She turned to Zuri. "You clearly love him to put up with all that's happened."

Zuri inhaled and released the breath. "I want to make this clear, Serena. I never saw Justice while you were married. Tasha brought him into our group after your divorce. Justice and I always confided in each other at school. When we reconnected, it was natural to fall into that pattern again." She paused. "That is, until the night before the wedding. I went to Justice's room to disclose how I felt. He had already told me about the contract and how he didn't love Tasha. I said he was making a huge mistake if he married her. I confessed I was in love with him." She lifted her shoulder. "You know what happened next."

"I asked Zuri why she didn't tell me sooner," Justice said. "We talked all night, and I decided to tell Tasha I couldn't marry her. In fact, I was headed to the bridal room when I saw you bolt from the reception hall."

"That's how you knew to run," Serena said. "You were outside the room."

"Yes." Justice hung his head. "I know they always blame the husband or boyfriend. I had to get out of there to think."

"I trust *Alfred* got enough time before we located you," Serena said with a straight face.

"Serena," Justice hissed.

"Hey, tell the truth now." Serena giggled.

"Don't worry." Zuri covered Justice's hand with her own. "I already know."

"What?" Justice's puzzled expression told Serena he had found the right woman.

"One more thing," Serena said. "When I stopped at your mom's, I saw you parked in the driveway. Was Zuri in the car?"

"Yes, she's remained at my side the entire time. The news outlets wouldn't leave me alone. We stayed at my parents' house, hoping no one would find us." Justice smiled. "Leave it to you, Serena."

"Yep." Serena nodded. "Leave it to me."

"Hi, Dad." Jade leaned over his shoulder and kissed his cheek. "Hi, Zuri." She glanced at Serena. "Jewel and I would like some time with Dad. Is that alright?"

"Absolutely," Serena answered.

"I want to tell him about your Christmas wedding."

"Jade!"

"He's invited, right, Mom?" Jade gazed at her a little longer than Serena liked.

"Yes," Serena answered. "If he wants to come."

"I'll be there with bells on, as they used to say." Justice chuckled. "Get it? Christmas? Bells?"

* * * *

"Let me get this straight," Jack said after they returned to their table. "You want to invite Bill Mitchell to the wedding?"

"Yes. I believe Bill and I have an understanding now. The invite will show I meant it."

"Okay, but you better run it by Nina," Jack replied. "The man is not her favorite."

"Did I hear my name?" Nina slipped into Jade's empty chair.

"I'll tell you later," Serena answered. "Thank you for this wonderful party."

"It was my pleasure," Nina said. "Have you started the wedding plans?"

"Nina! You are just as bad as the girls." Serena giggled. "They want us to get married at Christmas."

"I assume you want to wed in the gardens?" Nina lifted a brow. "By the pond?"

"You would need to shut down the gardens, Nina. I'd never ask you to do that."

"I'm offering."

"What about the second annual Christmas Market?" Serena asked.

"It ends before Christmas," Nina answered. "If you marry between Christmas and New Year's, it won't be a problem."

"You've thought of everything." Serena shook her head. "I can't win this argument, can I?"

"No." Nina smiled. "The tearoom and sushi restaurants are at your disposal. Use them as you wish."

"For cost?" Serena kidded.

"For nothing," Nina replied. "My wedding gift to you." She held up her hand. "Before you protest, I'm leaving."

Stunned, Serena turned to Jack. "My dream was to marry in the gardens. I never thought it would come true."

* * * *

Serena admired her wedding dress in the mirror. "What do you think, girls?"

"You are a vision, Mom," Jewel said. "The perfect, classic bride."

"But once you remove the lace jacket, it becomes the ideal dress for the reception," Jade replied.

"You're both correct." Serena glanced at the back and decided she had made the right choice.

Serena's fitted ivory gown hugged her curves as if made for her. *Well, it was. By my awesome designer friend, Mia.* The strapless sweetheart neckline gave it a romantic touch, while the corset-style bodice offered an elegant structure. She especially adored the lace-up back. For the ceremony, she wore a removable stretch beaded lace jacket that added a touch of sophistication. Its delicate beadwork caught the light and sparkled with every move. After one last look, she turned to her cousin and daughters and said in a soft voice, "I'm ready."

The wedding party shimmered in ruby red, a nod to her birthstone and favorite gem. Over the years, Jack had gifted her with jewelry bearing the stone. Now, on her wedding day, she wore the necklace and bracelet he had given her, a reminder of his love and thoughtfulness.

Sasha handed Serena her bridal bouquet. "It's beautiful, Serena. Jack wanted to design it for you, and he did a great job."

"He used our colors and theme to help him," Serena responded. "I didn't realize he paid that close attention." She giggled.

Jacqui had created a winter bouquet of red, burgundy, white, and champagne roses. Woodland greenery and pinecones surrounded the flowers with trailing vines of ivy and baby's breath cascading over the top. Identical flowers and same color décor would grace the reception tables.

"Ready?" Serena's Uncle Damian and Sasha's dad poked his head into the bridal room. "Everyone's seated, and the music has started." He adjusted his ruby red tie. "How do I look?"

"Handsome as ever, Daddy," Sasha replied. "Now, join Serena, and the three of us will start the procession."

"Mom," Jade said over her shoulder. "Don't be nervous. Nothing is going to happen."

Serena pressed her lips together. She couldn't speak or the tears she held back would roll down her cheeks.

"Serena, you look terrified," her uncle whispered. "I agree with Jade. All's well."

Serena erupted in laughter. "I'm not afraid, Uncle Damian. I am so happy, I could burst. This is my 'trying to hold back the happy tears' face."

"Well, change it up, girl, and replace it with the wonderful smile I love."

* * * *

Jacqui met Serena and her uncle at the Torii gate. "Everything is in place, Serena. I hope I've brought your vision to life."

"From what I've already seen, you've done an amazing job, Jacqui," Serena answered.

Serena immediately thought of Jacqui when she started to plan the wedding. No one else would do. She hired her as her florist and a consultant. Hoping to heal Jacqui's negative reputation, Serena promoted the flower shop on social media, posting photos and asking followers for their opinions.

Jacqui continually thanked Serena for the positive media attention and said she had no idea how to repay her, except to do the wedding at cost. Serena had refused the offer and said, "People are quick to forget, Jacqui, and move on to the next big thing. I'm happy to help." The proof became reality when Jacqui could hardly keep up with holiday and wedding orders.

"Evan and I are sitting in the back row, if you need anything," Jacqui whispered as she positioned Serena and her uncle at the start of the white runner leading to the altar.

Serena followed the runner with her eyes until she reached the wedding canopy. *Jack!* Her breath hitched. He looked incredibly handsome in his dark gray suit and ruby tie. Jacqui had used small pinecones and red berries against dark green foliage for the boutonnieres. Serena had wanted to mix Christmas with the outdoors as their theme and seeing it completed left her speechless.

Artificial pine trees surrounded the canopy and garland filled with berries, pinecones and tiny white lights wrapped around its poles. The staff had scattered more white lights and synthetic snow throughout the garden scenery, creating the feeling of being outdoors.

Uncle Damian offered Serena his arm and escorted her down the aisle. Serena and Jack had wished to keep the wedding small and intimate with a guest list of around fifty friends and family. She smiled at the friendly faces as she walked toward the man who had changed her life.

Her uncle placed Serena's hand in Jack's, kissed her cheek and took his place next to Robin and his wife. Serena met Jack's eyes, and all the worry dissolved. "Hi," she said.

"You look amazing," Jack replied.

The service was lovely, although Serena had to remind herself to concentrate and remember the details. When the pastor declared them man and wife, she was shocked it had ended so soon. "You may kiss the bride," he said.

Jack took Serena in his arms, and as his lips touched hers, snow began to fall. "The snow machine," Serena whispered to Jack. "I'd forgotten the hotel purchased one for the Christmas Market." She tilted her head back and let the tiny flakes come to a rest on her cheeks. "This is wonderful."

"May I present," the pastor said. "Mr. and Mrs. Jack Ando."

The guests cheered and clapped as Jack and Serena turned toward them.

"Look at all our family and friends," Jack said, smiling at Serena.

"Not just family and friends, Jack," Serena answered. "These are our people. Our village who helped us through so much."

With that, Jack wrapped his arm around Serena and guided her down the white runner, laughing and talking with guests as the gentle snow fell around them.

The End

Before You Go

Join Nancy's Mailing List and never miss a release!
nancypennick.com/nancy-pennick-newsletter-sign-up/
and visit me at:
nancypennick.com/

THANK YOU FOR READING

Did you enjoy this book?
I invite you to leave a review at your favorite book site,
such as
Goodreads, BookBub and Amazon.

DID YOU KNOW THAT LEAVING A REVIEW…

Helps other readers find books they may enjoy.
Gives you a chance to let your voice be heard.
Gives authors recognition for their hard work.
Doesn't have to be long. A sentence or two about why
you liked the book will do.

Continue Reading –

The Pearl Hotel Cozy Mystery Series
(Cozy Mysteries are stand-alone reads)

The Model's Last Pose (Book 1)
Gone with the Pearls (Book 2)
The Notorious Nutcracker Case (Book 3)
The Fatal Bouquet (Book 4)

Other Books by Nancy Pennick

**The $ecret Billionaire $ociety
Book 1-6 are stand-alone reads
(Contemporary Romantic Suspense)**

Chase (Book 1)
Nash (Book 2)
Finn (Book 3)
Beau (Book 4)
Gabe (Book 5)
Kade (Book 6)
The Elusive Mr. Smith (Book 7)
Smith's Revenge (Book 8)

**The Billionaire's Bride
(Contemporary Romantic Suspense Series)**

Vanessa (Book 1)
Grace (Book 2)
Charlotte (Book 3)
Tess (Book 4)
Lily (Book 5)
Mia (Book 6)

Waiting for Dusk Series (Young Adult)

Waiting for Dusk (Book 1)
Call of The Canyon (Book 2)
Stealing Time (Book 3)
Taking Chances (Short Story)
Broken Dreams (Prequel)

Twenty Nine Series (Young Adult)

29
29 Squared
29 Degrees
29 Forever

The Clan MacLaren Series
(Historical Romance)

My Highlander Husband (Book 1)
Donnach's Daughter (Book 2)
The Heart of the Emerald (Book 3)
Now and Forever (Book 4)

MacLaren Strong (Book 5)

Homecoming (Book 6)

ABOUT THE AUTHOR

For three decades, Nancy taught elementary school. She'd written short stories as a child, kept a diary and loved the writing process. After retiring, she hadn't set out to become an author, but when inspiration struck, she couldn't resist putting pen to paper. She now had time to follow her dream. Today her writing spans various genres, including young adult, historical romance, romantic suspense and cozy mysteries.

Nancy lives with her husband, Ron, and has a married son, who helps her with tech more than he likes! Plus, add in a wonderful daughter-in-law and grandson which makes her life complete.

www.ingramcontent.com/pod-product-compliance
Lightning Source LLC
Chambersburg PA
CBHW030133010826
48973CB00002B/543